THE BODY IN QUESTION

The bareheaded man stumbled toward me, his face distorted from two long, ragged red strokes from the blade, his jacket shredded, turning wet with blood. Then he dropped into the snow, face down. I tried to open the window now, but it was jammed. I ran into the bathroom, pulled Jill out of the shower, confused, naked, and wet.

"Look out there!" I said. "What do you see?"

"Nothing," she said.

I looked out the window. I didn't see anything either. Just the lake, the gazebo, and bridge, the cliffs, the evergreens, the snowy ground, as peaceful and unreal as a landscape painting you'd buy in a shopping mall.

The body was gone.

Tor books by Max Allan Collins

Nice Weekend For A MURDER

MAX ALLAN COLLINS

A TOM DOHERTY ASSOCIATES BOOK
NEW YORK

This is a work of fiction. All the characters and events portrayed in this book are fictitious, and any resemblance to real people or events is purely coincidental.

NICE WEEKEND FOR A MURDER

Cover art by Alan Ayres

A Tor Book
Published by Tom Doherty Associates, Inc.
175 Fifth Avenue
New York, N.Y. 10010

Tor® is a registered trademark of Tom Doherty Associates, Inc.

ISBN: 0-812-50138-1
Library of Congress Catalog Card Number: 86-5631

First Tor edition: June 1994

Printed in the United States of America

0 9 8 7 6 5 4 3 2 1

For Ed Gorman
best friend Mallory ever had

AUTHOR'S NOTE

Mohonk Mountain House is, of course, a real place; the Mohonk Mystery Weekend is a real event. But the mystery weekend in this book is a fictional one, as are the characters who take part in it—game-players, celebrity suspects, hotel staff, and the rest. It is my intention to summon *types* as opposed to doing *roman à clef* portraits of real people.

Likewise, *The Mystery Chronicler* is a fictional publication and is not patterned on any real magazine in the mystery (or any other) field.

My thanks to Faire Hart at Mohonk for her help, patience, and continual graciousness; to Peter Lewis and Kathe Mull for sharing their Sky Top memories; and to Don Westlake and Abby Adams for inviting me to one of the first Mohonk Mystery Weekends, where I had the honor of being the killer.

PART ONE
· · ·
Thursday

1
• • •

New York is a great place to visit, but I wouldn't want to live there. And it wasn't that great a place to visit, either, this time around.

When you make your living as a writer, at least as a writer of books, whether fiction or non-fiction or both, you must be resigned to the fact that occasional trips to New York City are a necessary evil. New York remains the hub of the publishing world, and if you don't go in now and then to remind your agent that you are more than a faceless voice attached to a bad phone connection, and to have long lunches with editors who must be similarly reminded, then you might as well have stayed in Iowa.

I might as well have stayed in Iowa. The two editors of mine I lunched with—for two respective houses— were glad to see me and had a lot of wonderful things to say about how nicely some of their other writers were doing. My books, unfortunately, weren't doing all that well. Oh, there'd been a flurry of activity when one of them sold to TV—and we even landed a book club sale; but a sale to paperback remained elusive and nobody was very optimistic. Including me.

And then my agent made my day ... in the Clint Eastwood sense, that is. He had just read the four-hundred-page change-of-pace manuscript I'd sent him a few weeks before—the book that would change my career, my "breakthrough book."

"Mallory, in good conscience," he said, "I can't even advise reworking this. It'd be a waste of bond paper. Put it in the drawer and try again."

My agent and I went way back—almost ten years. One of my teachers at a summer writers' conference had liked my first suspense novel well enough to write me a letter of introduction to this well-thought-of, if hard-nosed, agent, who had a stable of top-flight mystery writers. A hard, round ball of a man, Jake Kreiger was renowned for his lack of tact. As Curt Clark once said, "Jake Kreiger thinks tact is something you put on the teacher's chair."

I'd never run into this side of Jake Kreiger, not full-blast anyway; he always treated me kindly, if patronizingly. He had taken me on as a client based upon the manuscript I submitted to him way back when, thinking I was a promising kid. Trouble was, ten years later, at thirty-five years of age, I was still a promising kid to him. If I was still a kid, why were my temples turning gray?

So I fired him. He seemed surprised. He was a guy who landed million-dollar contracts for people, after all (not for me). He sat at his big desk in his little walk-down office on West End Avenue and looked, for a moment, like someone had punched him in his considerable stomach.

But he got over it quickly, handing me my thick manuscript with one hand and extending the other, offering it in a handshake, without standing, though he seemed sincere when he wished me the best of luck.

Now I was sitting on a bus, feeling like I was on my way to my draft physical. Anyway, that was the last bus ride I could remember being this depressed on. Of course, on that trip I hadn't been sitting next to a beautiful young woman, which was certainly an improvement over the naive Iowa farm boy I'd been sitting by then, a redheaded hick who was excited about getting a chance to "shoot some gooks." He had pronounced it "gucks," actually, but I didn't bother correcting him. Somebody else no doubt would. A gook, maybe.

But all of that was years ago. We'd both been to Vietnam, that naive farm boy and me—an only slightly less naive Iowa farm boy myself, come to think of it. I, at least, had made it back. And after several years of bumming around, in this job and that one, and the requisite bout with drugs, Haight Ashbury style, I'd ended up going home again, to Iowa, Thomas Wolfe's advice notwithstanding, where I took in some G.I.-Bill college and pursued my life's dream of being a writer. Specifically, a mystery writer.

And the dream had come true. Half a dozen books later, and here I was—a published, publishing writer, who had moved out of his house trailer in a questionable neighborhood into a house in an unquestionable neighborhood and even got to go to the Big Apple now and then to spruce up his career.

Which at the moment seemed to be over.

"This is only a setback," the beautiful woman sitting next to me said. Her name was Jill Forrest, and she was about the only positive part of my life I could think of at the moment. Well, my health was pretty good. Jill Forrest and my health. The rest you can have.

"That's what General Custer said," I replied. "Only a setback."

Jill pursed her lips in a wry little smile. She was a dark woman about my age, with short, black, spiky hair and cornflower-blue eyes and wardrobe by Kamali. She'd grown up in Port City, Iowa, like me, but had gone off to the big city, specifically NYC, and become a success. She'd landed back in Port City recently for a tour of duty at the local cable station. That's what she was doing these days: she set up new cable TV systems in cities and towns across the Great Plains, got 'em rolling, then mounted up and moved on to the next gunfight, like John Wayne. Her Port City mission was nearing its end, which was a sore point between us; this New York getaway together was a truce of sorts.

She pressed her hand against my sleeve. "Put those dreadful two days behind you," she said. "We've got a lovely weekend up ahead. We're just going to forget all about agents and editors and mystery writing."

"Jill," I said. "We're on our way to Mohonk, remember? Going to a mystery weekend to forget about agents and editors and mystery writing is like going to Disneyland to forget mice."

"We're going to have a good time, Mal, dammit. You promised."

"I know I did."

"Besides, maybe being around some other writers will be good for you."

"I'll find out I'm not the only one having problems, you mean? Because it's a tough business?"

"Yes. But more than just 'misery loves company'—you can get some advice about finding a new agent."

I *was* worried about that. Working out of Iowa meant I *had* to have an agent; without somebody looking after my interests in New York, my career would be just another Iowa crop that failed. But I'd had Kreiger from the very beginning. I knew no other agents, had no idea how to go about acquiring one.

"Maybe you're right," I said. "I can talk to Curt, at least. He might have some ideas. And Tom."

"Sure. This really is just a setback. In fact, I'd say it's for the better."

"For the better?"

"Yeah. Kreiger hasn't been doing much for you lately, has he?"

"No. He's been paying attention to his *successful* clients."

"I saw how he treats you. Like a kid. You need somebody who respects what you're doing. That new book of yours needs an agent who'll get excited about it."

"As opposed to one who suggests putting it in a drawer."

"Right. And as for your editors, they seem to like you and your work well enough. So your last couple of books haven't set the world on fire. So what? I'm sure they'll be open to new things from you. In fact, if you can't find an agent right away, you could show the new book directly to your editors."

"Yeah! Why not?"

She smiled again. "Why not indeed," she said.

Well, I felt a little better now. All I needed was a pep talk like that from her every ten minutes or so and I'd be fine.

In the meantime, the bus was moving along the New York State Thruway at a moderate pace; snow was coming down, traffic was slow, and the highway slippery. Me, I was homesick. Wishing I'd never agreed when my friend and, well, mentor Curt Clark invited me to be part of this mystery weekend. I'm not much for game-playing, after all. But the Mohonk people had paid for my plane ticket, in and out of New York City, meaning I could come in a few days early and squeeze in my business trip at their expense, as far as airfare was concerned. Which had made Mohonk seem like a great idea at the time.

I just hadn't counted on getting so bummed out (once a hippie, always a hippie) in New York. Visions of my agent being excited over my "break-through book," dreams of editors eagerly asking me to do even more books for them, for lots and lots of money, were replaced by the wet, gray sludge of reality that had settled in the space where my brain used to be.

So much for Jill's pep talk cheering me up.

I wished I was back in my little house with the river view in Port City, Iowa; sitting in front of the fireplace with Jill and me and no clothes at all, wrapped up in a blanket while the Iowa winter whistled outside and didn't get in, except through the occasional crack or cranny, and we didn't give a damn because we had the fire and the blanket and each other.

But I was still in New York—albeit not New York City. Jill and I—and I did have Jill, if not the fire and the blanket—were on our way to Mohonk Mountain House, a resort near New Paltz, upstate. I didn't know much about Mohonk, except that it was supposed to be a big, rambling old place, much in demand in the nicer months, and in the off-season it had been throwing some very successful, much imitated "mystery weekends."

A mystery weekend is a gathering at which mystery buffs and puzzle fanatics converge and, forming into teams, try to solve a mystery. At Mohonk, the plots were always concocted by a famous mystery writer, acted out by invited guests who are themselves nationally known mystery writers (the latter a category I barely fit, if my ex-agent and current editors were to be polled on the subject). On this very bus were a gaggle of mystery fans, chattering and flying high, almost giddy, on the idea of the weekend to come. Most of these people seemed fairly normal, although there were more Sherlock Holmes-style deerstalker caps than I'd ever encountered on one bus before.

None of my fellow mystery-writer guests seemed to be on this bus, which had departed New York late this afternoon, Thursday. Some of them were going by car, and others had taken an earlier bus. Both buses had left from Casablanca—an Italian restaurant on Twenty-second Street in Manhattan with a Bogart/mystery theme. Its owners, Carl and Millie Arnold, were among the most diehard Mohonk players, I'd heard. They were on the bus, already planning strategies. Apparently the two of them had been on the winning team for three years in a row.

Everybody on the bus was having a great time. It was a party atmosphere—except for yours truly, party-pooper extraordinaire. I sat looking out a frosty window at the New York State countryside whizzing by; it didn't look much different than the Midwest to me—more like Illinois than Iowa, maybe, but otherwise just generic winter countryside. Nor did New Paltz itself, as we moved down its main street of shops and restaurants, seem like anything other than the small college town it was. New York, strangely, seemed to be a part of America, once you got out of New York City, that is.

It was dark now, and we went over a bridge, took a right at the Mohonk sign, and started up the narrow blacktop road that climbed the mountain. The resemblance to the Midwest had come to an end. This was not a hill, which we have a few of in Iowa. This was a mountain. The real thing—rocky, big, and up. We stopped at a little rustic house, where the bus driver got out and checked in with a guard in a green blazer, who logged us in on a clipboard before allowing us on. Then the denseness of the snow-covered trees around us and the steepness of the climb settled in on us, as the bus finally began its upwardly mobile way through the darkness, creating an unreal mood. Almost a surreal mood.

"Agatha Christie, here we come," Jill said.

"More like Stephen King," I said.

Because suddenly the hotel was looming up before us like a monstrous movie set, a sprawling Victorian affair with towers and spires and gables and windows and windows and windows and balconies and balconies and balconies, wooden wings alternating with stone ones, a man-made cliff rising into the night sky.

Many of the players on the bus seemed unimpressed; they had been here before—they weren't naive Iowa farm boys, either. They were imperturbable Easterners, scurrying toward the entrance as bellboys in winter coats began transferring luggage from the underbelly of the bus onto carts.

I, on the other hand, stumbled off the bus with my mouth open and my eyes open and my mind reeling and just stood there.

"What the hell planet is this?" I asked nobody in particular.

"The planet Mohonk," nobody in particular responded, nobody in particular being Jill.

Some snow was falling, lightly, and the air was bitter cold. Everybody's breath was visible as we moved into the hotel and into warmth and another era. A Victorian era, where the woodwork was dark and polished, the halls were wide and carpeted, off of which were little parlors—sitting rooms—where the furniture was antique and plush, the lighting soft-focus and yellow. Wonders never ceased: frondy plants and fresh-cut flowers were everywhere; wide wooden stairways rose like a challenge to ignore those new-fangled elevators; here, a carved-wood and stone fireplace; there, a Chinese vase as tall as an eight-year-old child.

Which was fitting, because it was like being a child again, in your grandparent's house, where everything seemed to belong to yesterday, and where the rooms went on forever, and where the air was musty and fresh at the same time.

Jill saw it a different way; she cuddled to me and said, "It's like a huge haunted house . . . only we're the ghosts."

"Yeah," I said, grinning.

Because suddenly I wasn't depressed anymore.

Why? Hey, I'm a mystery writer, after all.

And this was a great place for a murder.

2

● ● ●

The lines at the check-in counter were long, but in their vicinity we ran into Tom Sardini, an old writer pal of mine, who was already checked in. He stood with us while we waited, so we at least could talk (or, as they say in New York, *schmooze*).

Old pal Tom wasn't all that old, really—in his early thirties—but we went back seven or eight years. Tom had written me my first fan letter, and I'd given him some help with some of his early manuscripts. He had gone on to be a successful writer himself—more successful than I actually, which is an excellent argument for not helping out aspiring writers.

Except that I liked both Tom and his stuff, anyway that which I'd been able to keep up with. He was widely known as the "fastest typewriter in the East," books flying out of his word-processor from his Brooklyn home in a blur of typescript, the royalty checks flying in the same way. He was making a small fortune (maybe not so small) by churning out adult westerns—his "Shootist" series of paperbacks was among the top three in the field; but his love was private-eye fiction: He was the founder of the Private-Eye Writers of America, and more important, his latest novel about ex-boxer-turned-P.I. Jacob Miles was so good I hated him.

Which is exactly what I told him, as I gave him a hug.

"This is Jill Forrest," I said, and Jill smiled at him and they shook hands. What kind of world is it, when two men hug, and a man and woman shake hands?

Tom, by the way, was five-ten, bearded, bespectacled, and a tad overweight, as befits a successful writer. I was leaner and taller and better-looking. Well, leaner and taller, anyway. He wore an off-white long-sleeved shirt and slacks; I was wearing jeans and a dark green sweatshirt that said "The Butler Did It," if it matters, winter coat slung over my arm.

"I've heard all about you," Tom said to Jill, taking in her slim figure with an appreciative smile. That figure was ensconced in a white and gray vertical-striped top and snug, black leather trousers, ball of white fur winter coat draped around her. She was a slightly snazzier dresser than me, as you have already gathered.

"I'd imagine you *have* heard about me," she said. "I've seen Mal's phone bills."

Tom and I shared long and expensive phone conversations into the wee hours; friendships in the writing game often require long-distance maintenance.

"And," Jill went on, showing Tom the ironic smile that was among the laundry list of reasons why I fell in love with her, "I've heard about you, too. Is it true you've written more books in your short life than Mal's read in his longer one?"

"Probably," Tom said.

Jill turned to me and squeezed my arm. "Look, I'll

get in line here, Mal, and get us checked in. You two go sit over there and insult each other for a while."

We took her advice, settling down on a velvet-cushioned settee. Various game-players were milling about expectantly, but here and there people sat and quietly talked—Tom and I, for instance, basking in the soft yellow lighting and warm, homey atmosphere of the old resort.

"Where's Anna?" I asked.

"She couldn't make it this trip," he said with a regretful little shrug.

"I haven't seen Anna since Bouchercon," I said. Anna was Tom's lovely, *zoftig*, Oriental spouse, who'd accompanied him to the annual mystery convention, held last year in San Francisco. "Hey! Wasn't she pregnant?"

"You really are the king of amateur detectives," he said. "She was only six months along, and you figured that out."

"My powers of observation are legend," I said. "Meaning, greatly exaggerated. So, what? She's home nursing a two-month-old?"

"Literally," Tom said, nodding. "Normally, I wouldn't do one of these things without her—but being invited to be part of Mystery Weekend at Mohonk is kind of an honor."

And it was. If I wasn't a friend of Curt Clark's, I wouldn't have been invited; I was just too small a fry in the mystery world to qualify. Curt, who was the latest of several top-rank mystery writers to head up the Mohonk Mystery Weekend, was "an acknowledged master of the comedy caper," as *The Mystery Chronicler* had put it.

"I see you're going to be speaking tomorrow afternoon," he said, referring to a program he held in one hand. "On 'Translating True Crime into Mystery Fiction.' "

"I haven't seen that yet," I said, meaning the program. "All I got in the mail from Curt was the suggested topic for my speech, and a cast list and description of my character in the mystery. Which I assume each of us playing a role got, so we could put together an appropriate wardrobe."

"Right," Tom said. "I play a tough private eye."

"Typecasting," I said.

"I guess. All I had to do was pack a trenchcoat and fedora and .38. Well, it's a full-scale replica of a .38, anyway. How about you?"

"I play a nerd," I said. "Sort of Pee-Wee Herman on the Orient Express. And no further comments on typecasting are necessary."

"All I can say is, *some* of us are *obviously* typecast. Did you get a load of who the murder victim is?"

"No. I mean, from the write-up Curt sent me about my character, I gather it's a critic."

"It sure is a critic," Tom grinned.

"Can I infer, then, that the role of critic is being played by some *real* critic?"

"You can. Care to guess who?"

"I don't remember seeing a critic on the guest list. . . ."

"Clark left that name off the list. He likes to play things cute, you know. That's what he's famous for, in those books of his—his wicked sense of humor."

"Who, then? The only critic *I* can think of that anybody might want to murder is that weasel Kirk Rath."

Tom beamed. "The very weasel in question."

Kirk S. Rath was, at the ripe old age of twenty-seven, easily the most famous and controversial critic in mystery circles. A smug, pedantic critic (his professed role model being John Simon), Rath was the editor and publisher of *The Mystery Chronicler*, published out of his home in Albany. This monthly magazine, famed for its in-depth interviews with mystery writers and its scholarly, yet entertaining, articles about the classic writers of both the drawing-room and tough-guy schools of mystery fiction, had been the surprise publishing success of the mystery world in recent years. Starting as a fanzine, *The Mystery Chronicler* had spread to the mystery bookstores and now was circulated to several of the major bookstore chains.

More important, it was widely circulated to libraries, and was having a big impact on which mysteries got bought by the libraries themselves, which, of course, was the major market for most hardcover mysteries.

For all its distinctions, however, *The Mystery Chronicler* was best known for one thing: the articulate but mean-spirited, often viciously personal criticism written by smug young Kirk Rath himself. Rath was currently tied up in no less than three libel cases, all stemming from his personal attacks upon various mystery writers.

"Brother," I said. "I don't know if I share Curt's sense of humor on that one. Every guest he's invited has reason to hate Rath."

"Including you."

"Yeah, he's fileted me a few times. And you, too."

"He *really* hates my work," Tom said, rolling his eyes.

" 'Sardini also writes adult westerns. Perhaps the prolific Mr. Sardini should stick to sagebrush and sex; his private-eye 'yawn' features a dim-witted detective who may be the most singularly uninteresting character in mystery fiction.' "

"Don't tell me you memorize bad reviews."

"They sear into my brain like a branding iron, as we cowboy writers from Brooklyn like to say. So . . . what did Rath say about you, Mal?"

"Which time?"

"Last time."

"I don't remember."

"Try."

"Umm, it might've been something like 'Mallory writes fictionalized accounts of real-life cases, and this latest is his most unengaging, unconvincing mock-up of all—thin on character, weak on basic storytelling skills.' "

"Yeah," Tom said. "I don't let bad reviews get to me, either."

Jill came over with our room key and said, "We're on the ground floor. I'd been hoping for one of those rooms with balconies and a view, but what the hell."

"I'm just down the hall from you," Tom said to her as he and I stood. "So my view isn't any better."

"Maybe Kirk Rath'll let us borrow his view," I said. "No matter what floor he's on, it's bound to be aloof."

"The room's this way," Jill said, gesturing; she'd had enough snappy patter and milling around. "I want to freshen up before dinner."

We told Tom we'd see him in the dining hall, and I followed Jill around a corner, down a wide corridor, subdued wallpaper and polished woodwork all around; it was one of those endless halls like in the movie version of *The Shining* (Stephen King again—he's everywhere) and I half expected that little kid to come pedaling his Big Wheel around the corner at us.

But he didn't and we finally found our room—64—and Jill worked the key in the lock, saying, "Tom seems like a nice guy."

"Yeah, sure," I said. "And he's probably written another book since we saw him last."

We stepped inside. The room was small—make that cozy—but it had its own polished-wood and brick fireplace with a fresh supply of firewood nearby. Our bags awaited us as well. The walls were papered in vertical stripes of yellow shades and the ceiling was high and the window looked out on a patch of snowy ground beyond which was the white frozen lake. A wooden, Japanese-style walkway bridge spanned a near section of the lake, from one ledge of rock to another, with a gazebo at midway point; the wooden bridge did not at all obscure the view of the lake, beyond which rock ledges rose, as well as towering evergreens, distinct and distinctly unreal in the blue-gray moonlight.

But back in the room we had a problem.

"Twin beds," we said.

"There must be some mistake," I said.

"Maybe it's because we're not married."

"If it comes to that, I'm ready for a ceremony at sea. Where's the captain of this ship?"

"Wouldn't that be your friend Curt Clark?"

I paced between the beds. "When I made the arrangements with Curt, I told him I was bringing a female companion. I figured he would've guessed I didn't mean my Aunt Mabel."

"If you had an Aunt Mabel."

"If I had an Aunt Mabel," I said, and then, in mid-pace, I noticed something else that wasn't there.

"Where's the goddamn TV?" I said.

Jill poked around, looking in this corner, and that one; and in the bathroom, and she even, I swear to God, looked under the nearest bed.

"There doesn't seem to be one," she said.

"How do they expect me to watch 'Hill Street Blues'?"

"Somehow I don't think they do."

"What the hell else am I supposed to do with my Thursday nights in Iowa?"

"We're not in Iowa, anymore."

"They got TVs in New York," I said, irritably, "even

upstate," and went for the phone on the nightstand between the beds. Only there wasn't one.

"There isn't even a damn *phone*," I said. "Maybe if I go down to the front desk, they'll provide me with two tin cans and a long piece of string!"

"Cool it, lover," Jill said, pointing to the table next to her. "There's a phone here by the window."

And there it was. It had been right in front of me before and I hadn't noticed, so caught up in the view of the lake and mountains and such had I been.

"It's on a long cord," Jill said. "Want to move it over to the nightstand?"

"No," I said, joining her, dialing O. "All I want is my TV and a double bed."

"I like a man who knows what he wants."

"Curt Clark's room, please," I told the operator, and waited. I looked around the room some more, waiting for Curt to come on the line.

"If I got to pay a little extra myself," I said, "I *am* going to get my double bed and TV. I'm a juggernaut on this one, kid."

She gave me a thumb's up. She worked for a cable company. She believed in TVs. Double beds, too, for that matter.

The phone was ringing in Curt's room and in my ear and it would have gone on forever, I guess, if I hadn't hung up.

I stood. I spread my hands and said, not without a little desperation, "How do they expect us to have any fun in a room with twin beds and no TV?"

Jill shrugged expansively. "It's a mystery to me. . . . But then this is a mystery weekend, isn't it?"

"Come on," I said, taking charge, heading for the door. "If I know Curt, he'll be down in the bar. We can get this thing straightened out."

My hand was on the door but I stepped back; somebody had thumped my doorknob with a knock. Okay, then. I was game; I opened the door.

Curt Clark was standing there, with a big grin on his face—and where else did you expect it to be?

He moved in past us, a good-looking, rangy guy in his late forties, with thinning blond hair and dark-rimmed glasses; he was wearing a sports coat with patched elbows, and corduroy trousers.

"Ah, good!" he said, gesturing about him. "You got one of the nice rooms."

"The nice rooms?"

"Well, they're *all* nice, but they don't all have fire-places. That's cute, don't you think?"

"Yeah, uh ... it's cute."

Curt turned to Jill and said, "And you must be ..."

"Mal's Aunt Mabel," she said, smiling, shaking his hand.

He didn't get the joke, but he knew an inside joke when he saw one and laughed a little anyway. "Funny," he said, "I figured you for this Jill Forrest person Mal's always raving about."

Tom Sardini wasn't the only reason my phone bills were thicker than my latest novel.

"That's me," she said. "I have to admit I haven't read any of your books yet ..."

"You're in good company," Curt said, smiling some more.

"But I intend to soon," she said. "I'm not really a mystery fan—"

Curt waved a hand in the air. "Me, either!"

"—though I've started to read a few, on Mal's recommendation. I'm enjoying them."

"Let me guess," Curt said, stalking our room, checking it out, peering out the window at the icy lake. "He's feeding you Roscoe Kane intravenously."

This time I smiled. "I haven't hit her with any Kane, yet. I'm starting her off on Hammett and Chandler."

"Good, good," Curt said, planting his feet in one place. "In twenty or so years he'll have you worked up to me."

"Oh no," Jill said. "You're coming up next ... right after Mickey Spillane."

Curt laid a hand on his chest. "Rating right after the Mick on Mal's reading list is a high compliment indeed. This doesn't prevent me from being horrified, of course. Speaking of which, isn't this place *something*? *This* is where they should've filmed *The Shining*!"

Him again.

"Actually, Curt," I said tentatively, "we were wondering about the twin beds ..."

"All the rooms have twin beds," he said dismissively.

"Well, uh, what about the television?"

"There aren't any televisions. Why, are you still watching *television*? Nobody watches television. I thought you were a *writer*, for Christ's sake."

"This place does have me a little confused," I admitted. "Look, let's go down to the bar. I'll buy you a drink and—"

"There's no bar," Curt said.

I laughed. "I could have sworn you said—"

"There's no bar," he said. "I said that, yes. That's because there's no bar."

I looked at Jill; she looked at me.

"This place is owned and operated by Quakers," he said.

"Quakers?" I said.

"Quakers?" Jill said.

"Quakers," Curt said. "You know—like the oats."

"Nixon was a Quaker," I said. "He drank."

"Not here," Curt said. "The hotel—which insists on calling itself a 'mountain house,' by the way, because the Quakers who originated the place didn't want to own anything so decadent as a 'hotel'—has no bar, the rooms have no television, and there are no double beds. With that in mind, feel free to have as much fun as you want." He checked his watch. "They're serving supper now."

"They do have *food* here, then?"

Curt grinned. "Sure, after you say grace," he said, and went out.

I followed, and Jill hesitated at the door, locking up, then followed me.

"I'll show you to the dining hall," he said. Then he nodded to room sixty-two as we passed and said, "We're neighbors, by the way. Feel free to knock for a cup of sugar anytime Kim and I aren't in the room."

Kim was Curt's wife, a lovely woman in her late twenties, an actress.

"How did you do in the city?" Curt asked me.

"Well, I don't have an agent anymore."

"Jake Kreiger finally got to you, huh? What the hell, you're due for a change."

Jill said, "Maybe you could talk to *your* agent for Mal—"

I said, "Jill, please—"

Curt grinned. "My agent's Jake Kreiger. Lack of tact doesn't bother me much—I'm a native New Yorker."

"Woops," Jill said.

"Mal, forget all that career crap—the point of this place is getting away from it all," Curt said, gesturing with both hands, walking fast. He seemed a little keyed up from all the responsibility. "Away from the modern world into something more peaceful."

As he said this, three women in deerstalker caps scurried by, chattering like magpies.

"Right," I said.

"Of course," Curt said, as we followed him up the wide stairs to the dining hall, "there's nothing like a little old-fashioned murder to liven things up a bit. . . ."

3

...

The dining room was an expansive, pine-paneled affair with an open-beamed ceiling that went up a couple of stories, and would have seemed austere if not for the usual Mohonk soft yellow lighting from chandeliers. The scores of small tables with white cloths and hard wooden chairs were attended by young men, in gold jackets, and young women, in black dresses with white aprons, whose serving counters were built around support beams, coffee steaming, condiments awaiting someone's need. It was like a Protestant church with food.

And the food was good, if surprisingly no-frills Midwestern in style. I as reminded of the many fine family-style restaurants at the Amana Colonies back in Iowa, where bowl upon bowl of basic but quite wonderful food is brought to your table till you say "when"; and those of us from farm stock take our good sweet time about saying "when," too. Mohonk was the same dang deal—homemade bread and rolls, fruit, steaming parsley potatoes and mixed vegetables, and your choice of two meats, tonight fried chicken and roast beef, medium rare.

After two days in New York, lunching and supping with editors and my erstwhile agent at expensive hole-in-the-wall Manhattan eateries (I've always wanted to use that word in a sentence) serving haute cuisine and sushi and the like, my middle-brow, middle-west taste buds were delighted to greet something so plainly, so purely *food.*

The heavy-set gentleman sitting opposite me—a barrel-chested man with short gray hair, gray eyes, and a startling tan, rather spiffily dressed in a blue blazer and open-collared peach-color shirt with a single gold chain at his throat—seemed to agree with me. He, too, was chowing down.

We had already introduced ourselves—he was Jack Flint (and I was Mallory, remember?) and I said I was pleased to meet him, and I was: he was one of my favorite writers in the genre, one of the handful of modern "tough-guy" practitioners that I kept up with.

Flint was in his mid-forties—and was that rarity among mystery writers: He had at one time been a private detective in what we laughingly refer to as "real life." His detective novels were private-eye procedurals, dealing with such real P.I. practices as skip tracing and process serving, and were written in a beautifully understated manner worthy of Joe Gores.

"How does this compare to California-style fare?" I asked, knowing Flint was from San Francisco.

The pleasant features of his rather full face all seemed to smile at once, particularly the gray eyes. "It beats sprouts," he granted me.

His wife, Janis, sitting next to him, was an unassumingly attractive blonde, wearing a white, yellow and orange print dress and no makeup. She seemed to be eating only salad and such.

"This menu does play hell with a vegetarian," I said to her.

She smiled shyly and nodded.

Jill, next to me, said, "I'm something of a vegetarian myself, only I allow myself chicken and fish."

Also hot dogs, tacos, and pepperoni pizza, if truth be told, but why spoil the spell?

Janis Flint said, "I eat fish too." And smiled. She seemed almost painfully shy, but if anybody could bring her out, it would be Jill.

In fact, Jill began trading information with Janis—who, it turned out, was a grade-school teacher and who was involved in educational television, which gave cable maven Jill something to latch onto—while I questioned Flint.

At first I unashamedly told him about my agent problems, and he recommended his own guy—"He's British and *long* on tact'—and wrote the info down on the back of one of his cards, telling me to feel free to mention his name. He had made a friend forever.

Actually, I was a little embarrassed by his straightforward kindness and, so, we ate in silence for a while after; silence but for Jill talking with Janis, who had loosened up some. I told you so.

"Haven't seen a book from you in a while," I said to him, finally.

Flint took time out from the breast of chicken he was working on to shrug and reply. "I'd like to, but the money is so much better in Hollywood."

"Why, uh, have you moved there . . .?"

He smiled. "No, but I've been writing for them. A couple of 'Mike Hammer's and a 'Magnum,' last season; a 'Riptide' coming up. And the screenplay for *Black Mask*."

Black Mask was Flint's most famous novel—a historical fantasy about a murder committed at a dinner attended by all the famous pulp writers of the thirties; Raymond Chandler and Dashiell Hammett team up to solve the crime, which turns out to have been committed by Carroll John Daly. A movie had been in the works for years; Spielberg himself had optioned it. Big bucks.

"Is that movie going to happen?"

He shrugged. "They're in so-called preproduction now. Spielberg has one of his film-school cronies on it. The shooting script doesn't have much to do with my book *or* my script."

"That must be disappointing."

"No. It's just Hollywood."

"Well, I sure hope your 'Case File' novels get going again."

He raised an eyebrow. "After what the critics did to the last one, how *dare* I?"

"Don't be silly. The critics *love* your books."

"Well, the last 'Case File' didn't even rate a *New York Times* review ... and that little S.O.B. Rath savaged it. Library sales were pitiful. The paperback bailed us out a little."

"Uh ... I guess you aren't aware that ..."

"Rath is an 'honored' guest here? Yes, I am. Curt warned me; he knows how I feel about Rath. I came anyway."

"How *do* you feel about Rath?"

"Let's just say I wish *I* was the murderer."

I remembered some of Rath's reviews of Flint's books. Rath had called Flint misogynistic and psychopathic, because his most recent novel focused on a psychotic rapist (is there any other kind?) as narrator. It was a bold book, a chilling and distinctive performance, perhaps the best novel of its kind since Jim Thompson's

The Killer Inside Me. The latter sentence is my opinion, however—not Rath's. Rath trashed the novel and, by assuming the narrator's sensibilities, mirrored the author's, made the most unpardonable blunder in literary criticism.

"His *Mystery Chronicler* is probably the single major obstacle keeping me out of the book business," Flint said matter-of-factly.

"Is he that important?" Jill asked, her conversation with Mrs. Flint having gotten sidetracked as Flint and my discussion about Rath gathering steam.

"Yes," I said, nodding. "He's hurt me, too. My editor at Crime Club feels Rath's negative reviews may be keeping my series out of paperback."

"One reviewer?" Jill said. "That doesn't seem possible!"

Flint wiped his chin with a napkin and gestured with a thick hand with delicate fingers. "It's quite possible, Ms. Forrest."

"Jill, please."

"Jill. It's quite possible. Mysteries don't garner a lot of reviews, anyway ... only those bigger books that 'cross over,' 'break out of category,' as they say. Enough negative reviews in The *Mystery Chronicler* can break a career."

"That seems absurd," Jill said.

"Doesn't it," Flint said.

A waiter leaned in and refilled my iced tea glass. "Actually," I said, "most of the *Chronicler*'s reviewing is pretty even-handed. They favor no specific school, but single out what they see as the best work in every phase of the mystery."

"That's part of the problem," Flint said. "The *Chronicler* isn't as consistently tough as, say, *Kirkus*. It's just when they *do* do a negative review—and Rath almost always writes those himself—it's a devastating one."

Tom Sardini, who was sitting next to Janis Flint, looked up from his dessert—a portion of strawberry shortcake a story or so high—to comment, "Jeez, Jack, I thought you were one of Rath's *favorites*."

"I was for a while," Flint said with a rueful smile. "He really put me on a pedestal. Called me my generation's 'Hammett,' which is the kind of praise any writer in our field dreams to hear."

I laughed, only there wasn't any humor in it. "That's his classic approach. He singles somebody out for praise, builds 'em up over a period of time and, then, when he deems 'em too big for their britches, tears 'em down. Rath giveth, Rath taketh away. He's a Frankenstein who comes to resent all the monsters he's created."

"Your metaphor stinks," Mallory," Flint said, in a friendly way. "It's Rath who's the monster."

The table next to us was where Curt Clark and his wife Kim, an exaggeratedly pretty, rather *zoftig* brunette, were seated; so was another of the guest writers, my old friend Pete Christian, author of so many fine books on mystery movies. Curt rose and came over to check us out, apparently having overheard Rath's name mentioned.

"Am I forgiven yet for inviting your Rath?" Curt asked us, eyes atwinkle, leaning in between Mr. and Mrs. Flint. "And that's a pun, ladies and gentlemen."

"Aren't puns a capital crime in New York state?" Flint asked.

"I wish a bad pun were *all* that Kirk S. Rath was," I said. "It's easy for you to take this lightly, Curt. I've never seen him give *you* a bad review."

Curt shrugged. "I don't much care. I don't read reviews."

"Really?" I asked.

"Not more than three or four times," he said. "How

do you like the food? It's not fancy, but there's plenty of it."

Jack Flint smiled up at Curt and said, "Do you always answer your own questions?"

"Do I? I don't think so."

Tom Sardini tore himself away from his strawberry shortcake long enough to say, "And where *is* the ever-popular Mr. Rath?"

"He's already eaten," Curt explained. "The dining room's been serving since six o'clock, and it's almost eight now."

"He wasn't on our bus," Jack said.

"Or ours," I said.

"He drove up in his own car," Curt said. "Have you ever met Rath?"

The question seemed to be posed to me, so I answered it: "Yeah, a couple of times. He was at the last couple Bouchercons, and I ran into him at an Edgar Awards dinner a few years back. He was nasty, but he lacks sting when he isn't in print. Strikes me more as immature and ... well, naive, than anything else."

"*I've* never met him," Jill said. "And I'm dying to."

Curt checked his watch. "Well, you'll get your chance in twenty minutes. That's when the game begins, downstairs in the big parlor. I know drawing-room mysteries ain't the style of you hardbitten private-eye writers, but just do your best to fit in."

Curt smiled and returned to his table, while a waitress set my strawberry shortcake in front of me. The berries were blood-red and juicy. Jill was already working on hers. Even the thought of Kirk Rath couldn't kill our appetites.

4

• • •

Outside the dining room, Pete Christian caught up with us. Pete was a warm, enthusiastic man, an eternal precocious kid wrapped up in a slightly stocky, vaguely disheveled, middle-aged package. In his rumpled Rumpole-of-the-Bailey suit, he looked like the lone survivor of a town hit by a tornado—a survivor whose only comment was, "What wind?"

"Mal," he said, eyes dancing behind dark-rimmed glasses, moustache twitching with his smile, "it's so good to see you. I've been meaning to call."

We shook hands and patted each other's shoulders and grinned at each other.

"Jill, this is Peter Christian. He wrote that book on the Charlie Chan movies I loaned you, remember?"

"That was a terrific book," Jill said, pumping his hand.

"Are you a mystery fan?" Pete asked her, pumping back.

"Not really. But I always liked Charlie Chan movies on the late show, when I was a kid."

"My dear, you're *still* a kid, but a kid with very good taste. I think Sidney Toler's underrated, don't you?"

"Definitely," she said. "But then I even like the Roland Winters ones. I like all those old movies."

"Well, then you're in luck; I'm in charge of the film program here, and we're showing three of the best ones . . . including *Charlie Chan at Treasure Island*."

Her face lit up. "Ah! The one about magicians, with Cesar Romero."

"Yes! And for the Warner Oland purists we'll be leading off with *Charlie Chan at the Opera*."

"Boris Karloff is wonderful in that," Jill said.

Pete gave me a mock reproving look. "I thought you said she wasn't a mystery fan! She knows more about mysteries than you do."

"I now pronounce you man and movie buff," I said. "You two can go trivially pursue yourself all weekend, for all I care. As far as I'm concerned, nostalgia ain't what it used to be."

We had been moving—Pete's a restless type, and when you talk to him he paces, chainsmoking—and were now at the mouth of the Parlor, the massive capital "P" parlor which was really a lecture hall and would double as the screening room. Both the dining hall and the Parlor were on the so-called first floor (the real first floor being designated as the ground floor, in the European manner).

"Are you going to be a suspect or a player?" Peter asked Jill.

"Neither," she said.

"I hope you're not here for a rest," he told her, wagging a finger. "This place will be a virtual madhouse for the next forty-eight hours. The Mohonk Mystery Weekenders take their mystery very seriously."

"I thought they were here for fun," she said.

"You'll find all sorts of brilliant professional people here," Pete said. "Intensely competitive types in their work—and in their play. They're out for blood, my dear."

"I hope it doesn't get unpleasant."

"If you're a student of human nature, you'll have a fine time. Anyway, I don't take this as seriously as some do, yet I've guessed the murderer seven out of nine times."

"How many of these have you attended?"

"All but one. This is my first time as a suspect."

"I'm impressed," she said.

"Mal," Pete said, "some time this weekend, we must get together. There's something we need to work on."

"What's that?"

"I've been lobbying to get a Grand Master's Award for Mickey Spillane."

"From the Mystery Writers of America? Is there any hope of that happening?"

Pete shrugged elaborately, did a little take, put out a cigarette, found another, and got it going. "I don't know," he admitted. "Spillane's never joined the MWA, and some of the members feel he's snubbed them."

"Well, a lot of them have snubbed *him*. You can't deny his influence on the genre, even if you don't like his work. He deserves that recognition."

"I agree, most heartily. I just wondered if you'd help me draft a letter on the subject to the proper committee chairman."

"I'd love to."

"There *is* a problem with that," a voice said. Not my voice. Not Pete's.

We turned to look at the source of the voice, which was across from us on a bench. A small, thin man in his late twenties in a gray three-piece suit with a dark blue tie snugged tight in the collar of a light blue button-down shirt sat with his legs crossed, ankle on knee, arms crossed, smirking. Handsome in an angular way, he was blue-eyed, pale as milk, with carefully-coiffed longish blond hair. He had paid more for that haircut than I had for my last three.

"And what problem is that?" I asked.

"Mickey Spillane is a cretin," Kirk S. Rath said. "He is—if you'll pardon my crudity—a shitty writer."

Jill swallowed and looked at me, knowing I wouldn't take that well.

"If you'll pardon my crudity," I said, "*you're* full of shit."

And I turned back to Pete, who was, after all, the person I'd been having my private conversation with, and said, "When do you want to draft that letter? Let's not make it tonight. I'm pretty wasted from two days in NYC, and that bus trip . . ."

Rath was standing next to me now; I hadn't seen him come over. It was like a jump cut in a film.

"I don't see any reason to get personal, Mallory," Rath said.

I sighed. "You referred to a writer I respect—a man I've met and like—as a cretin. That strikes me as personal. Sort of like the personal conversation you inserted your opinion into."

He smirked again. "Now I'm being accused of intellectual rape."

"Hardly," I said. "I don't think you could get it up."

The smirk dissolved into a sneer.

"You have a decided suicidal streak, don't you, Mallory?"

"Why, because you'll pan my next book? As opposed to those glowing things you've said about me in the past? Go to hell, Kirk."

"You're rude and you're crude."

"And I'm a hip talkin' dude. What do you know, Kirk? We're rappin'! Now go away."

Rath looked at Pete, sharply, and said, "I don't like your choice of company, Christian."

"I don't like people who barge into private conversations," Pete said, with some edge.

Jill glanced at me, and I glanced at her.

Rath pointed a finger at Pete like a manicured gun. "You're vulnerable, too, my friend."

"I'm not your friend," Pete said. "I haven't forgotten what you did to C.J. Beaufort."

"What *I* did? Beaufort wrote very bad books, and killed himself. I had nothing to do with either."

"You *destroyed* him in print!" Pete was shaking a fist. "It shattered him!"

Rath ignored Pete's fist and laughed. "Writers are public figures; their work is submitted for public consumption. If they can't take the heat, they should get the hell out of the literature."

Pete was trembling; really worked up. "C.J. Beaufort was a kind, gentle man . . . and he was my friend!"

I stepped in between Pete and Rath. "I hate to break up this little family reunion, but we were all due downstairs about five minutes ago."

Rath shook his head, said, "You people are pathetic," and clomped down the nearby stairs.

"So that was Kirk S. Rath," Jill said, shaken.

"Himself," I said, feeling a little battered myself.

"I should have thrown him down the stairs," Pete said as we started down them. He was huffing with anger.

"I shouldn't have baited him," I said, regretting having ignited the scene between them. "I *was* rude and crude."

"Nonsense! We were talking and he butted in. That

arrogant little bastard. You knocked him down a peg or two."

"Yeah, right. That brings his ego almost down into the stratosphere."

Jill said, "He's amazing. Did you see his eyes?"

"What about them?" I asked.

"He's certifiable," she said. "He's a sociopath."

"He doesn't feel a shred of remorse over Beaufort's suicide," Pete said, a little amazed.

"Kirk Rath isn't a sociopath," I said. "He's just immature. He's an arrested adolescent. Or is that an adolescent who should be arrested?"

"You're too easy on him," Pete said, shaking his head, lighting up another cigarette.

"I think he truly doesn't understand why his criticism is taken so personally," I said. "He's a permanent grad student, dazzled by his own William F. Buckley vocabulary and arch prose style."

"He knows about the power of the pen," Pete said, nodding, "but he doesn't understand the responsibility that goes with it."

"Maybe that's why everybody and his duck is suing him," Jill offered.

"C.J. Beaufort can't sue him," Pete said.

And he walked on into the large downstairs parlor where the game players were assembling.

Jill looped her arm in mine. "What's the story on this guy Beaufort?"

"I don't know all the details," I said. "Beaufort was a pulp writer, dating back to the *Black Mask* days. He was an alcoholic. He had some success in the forties, then faded, and wrote paperbacks under many names, for many years. He had some vocal fans, Pete among them, but mostly he was thought of as a solid pro, a journeyman, nothing special. Till Rath."

"What did Rath do?"

"From the beginning of the *Chronicler*, Rath used Beaufort as the consummate example of a talentless hack . . . really harped on it, making 'Beaufort' a virtual synonym for 'hack.' "

By then I was whispering, because we were moving into the big, low-ceilinged chestnut-and-glass parlor known as the Lake Lounge, where several hundred mystery fans were sitting on the floor like Indians. A few were leaning against walls and beams and just generally cramming themselves in. Curt Clark and his wife and the other mystery-writer guests (and spouses and companions) were lined up along one side, and the mostly seated game-players were watching Curt and company with rapt attention.

Rath stood leaning against a beam, his expression foul. Cynthia Crystal, whose urbane drawing-room mysteries had led one critic to dub her "the American Agatha," was trying to hold a conversation with Rath. She was smiling, being very friendly, laughing in a brittle manner that Rath didn't seem to be buying. Cynthia was a lanky, fortyish blonde, in a chic-looking charcoal suit ("Halston," Jill whispered), and she was smoking nervously. I knew her pretty well, and liked her. I knew less well her live-in lover, Tim Culver, whose presence here surprised me.

Culver, a bearded man with wire-rim glasses and a quiet demeanor, looked something like Woody Allen's older, better-looking brother. He was, in fact, Curt Clark's older, not necessarily better-looking brother, older by about a minute that is. They were twins. Not identical twins, though the physical resemblance was strong. Otherwise they had little in common. Oh, they were both mystery writers, but Curt wrote comedy, whereas Culver was an exponent of the tough-as-nails school. Where Curt was a witty, life-of-the-party type, Tim was rather dour. He stood slumped against another beam, a drink in his hand (he'd brought his own—Quakers, remember), in a tan corduroy jacket and jeans and an open-at-the-neck plaid lumberjack shirt.

"That's a shock," I whispered to Jill.

We were standing next to Jack Flint and his wife; Tom Sardini was chatting with Pete, the two of them standing as far away from Rath as they could and still be a part of the group. The crowd was noisy, eager for Curt to get started.

"What's a shock?" Jill asked.

"I knew Cynthia was a guest, but I didn't know Tim Culver would be."

"Who's Tim Culver?"

I nodded toward him, slightly. "That guy. He's only the best writer alive in the Hammett tradition. He makes Elmore Leonard look wordy."

"So why are you shocked?"

"He and Curt are brothers. Curt's last name is Culver, too. Clark was his mother's maiden name or something."

"Yeah, so? What's surprising about one brother inviting another brother?"

"They hate each other," I said.

Jill blinked.

"Oh," she said.

"Go away!" somebody said.

The crowd was noisy enough that the outburst didn't get heard by anybody but us mystery writers and the first row or so of game-players. But those of us who heard it were startled.

It was Kirk Rath, speaking to Cynthia Crystal.

Cynthia Crystal, the critically acclaimed, Edgar-award-winning author, whose biography of Dashiell Hammett had been called by Kirk Rath himself "definitive and masterful."

"Don't suck up to *me*, lady!" Rath snapped.

Cynthia was taken aback; she swallowed, said nothing. Now, Cynthia has a sharp enough tongue—she's a cool, bitchy number when she wants to be. But the rude, powerful young Mr. Rath had knocked her back.

"I was just making conversation," Cynthia said, still stunned. "Trying to be friendly . . ."

"Why?" he said archly. "What's your motive? This is the *mystery* world—there's *always* a motive."

Culver moved away from his beam and joined this little Edward Albee one-act.

"You shut up," he said to Rath.

Rath looked at him with cold anger.

"Your . . . lady, here, has been trying to get on my good side," Rath said. "I resent that. Just because her last novel got a less than favorable review from us doesn't mean her next attempt won't be treated impartially."

"Who said it wouldn't be?" Cynthia said, genuinely confused. "I was just making some small talk. We're both guests here . . ."

"Just keep your distance," Rath said. "Both of you."

Culver gripped both of Rath's lapels and lifted the little critic off the ground. Culver said nothing at all, just looked at the wide-eyed Rath a moment, and set him back down. Rath swallowed, his mouth suddenly dry it would seem, and apparently couldn't find anything nasty or witty or trenchant to say to Culver, who slipped an arm around Cynthia's shoulder and escorted her a few paces away, near Jill and me.

"Hi, Cynthia," I said.

She hadn't noticed me before; she had tears in her eyes, which wasn't common for this cool cookie, but she flung herself in my arms and gave me a hug.

"Mal," she said. "Mal, it's great to see you. How long has it been?"

"Two years, I guess. The Chicago Bouchercon.

Looks like your next review in the *Chronicler*'s going to be a doozie."

She laughed. "That Rath's a prize, isn't he? At least we get to kill him this weekend."

Culver said, "That boy's a born murder victim."

"He wouldn't make it past the first commercial of 'Perry Mason,'" I agreed. "Too bad this is reality."

The first few rows of players were abuzz; some had witnessed Rath's outburst, and others were hearing about it via the grapevine.

"All part of the show, kids," Curt Clark said, stepping out before the crowd, a clipboard in hand. He adjusted his glasses and glanced at the top sheet and said, "Many of you have been here before, but for the newcomers let me explain that you've been divided into teams. We've already passed the badges out, some of you are wearing them already, I see—fifteen or so players per team. We've kept couples together, but otherwise the teams were randomly selected. We'll have a lot of fun this weekend, and not all of it involves the mystery you're going to *attempt* to solve . . ."

Smiles and murmurings followed the word "attempt," rolling like a wave across the crowd.

"Our honored guests will be playing roles in the little melodrama I've concocted," Curt went on, "and you will have at them only *twice*. On both Friday—that's tomorrow—and Saturday—that's the day after tomorrow—you'll have a one-hour interrogation period, during which members of your teams can grill the various suspects. You'll know them by their badges, which will be clearly labeled 'suspect.' Now, they all have to tell the truth, at all times . . . all of them except the *murderer*, that is."

Laughter.

"And on Sunday morning, your teams will present *their* versions of how to solve *The Case of the Curious*

Critic. There will be two awards—one for the team coming closest to the solution as I've devised it; and another for most imaginative presentation. And, yes, it is possible for one team to win both awards, though it hasn't happened yet. The members of the winning teams will be presented with a reservation for the *next* Mohonk Mystery weekend."

That brought applause, even though the reservations were *not* all-expenses-paid; they were in fact no-expenses-paid—but the Mohonk Mystery Weekend sold out every year in less than an hour, and hundreds, to put it conservatively, were shut out accordingly.

Curt explained that the weekend would also include movies, lectures, and a dance; he then began to give each of us guests a gracious introduction.

Finally he got to Kirk S. Rath.

"And now," Curt said, "allow me to introduce the critic we love to hate, a man who truly needs no introduction—our very own murder victim, *The Mystery Chronicler*'s Kirk S. Rath."

There was considerable applause, even whistles, for Rath, who did have his public. You couldn't take that away from him. He was seen by many mystery fans as daring, iconoclastic. I found him a terrible, pretentious writer, but had to admit he could be entertaining in his boldness.

When the applause died down, Rath stepped forward; none of us had spoken after our intros, but Rath, it seemed, had something to say.

"I think you people are pitiful," he said, speaking not only to the other professionals/guests, but to the fans/players before him. A sea of smiles ebbed.

"If you'd ever read an issue of the *Chronicler*," he said, "you'd know I've striven to make the mystery something that could be taken seriously, that could be viewed as literature, not mere pulp. Now, I'm not without a sense of wonder, a sense of fun . . . and I thought I'd enjoy this weekend. But what I see here—this assemblage of alternately rude and fawning writers, this horrific assortment of starry-eyed fans and drooling 'gamers,' armed with pocket calculators and deerstalker caps—is perhaps the most nauseating sight I've ever had the misfortune to witness. You're denigrating, belittling, a serious American art form, a form perhaps second only to jazz in its cultural worth—*at its best*, that is, as opposed, say, to its nadir as represented by the likes of such small fish as Mr. Sardini and that pretentious poseur who signs his work only 'Mallory.' "

Every jaw in the house had dropped to the floor.

Except Rath's, which was still churning: "I have a certain respect for the work of Curt Clark. So when he approached me, I agreed to attend this charade—only to discover when I arrive that I'm to play a cruel parody of myself, and *then* to be 'murdered,' to play a corpse, to be what so many of you wish I truly were: dead. Well, you'll have to find yourself another body. I've had enough of this nonsense. I'm not playing."

And Rath walked through the crowd's Red Sea, which parted for his Moses, and was gone.

5

• • •

Curt calmed the crowd by pushing the air with his palms and smiling.

"We all know Kirk's a shade temperamental, but I'll do my best to catch him and convince him to stick around for the fun. In the meantime, Pete Christian has a movie scheduled for about half an hour from now, in the Parlor upstairs. I think you'll find it apropos."

Pete stepped forward and said, "It's *Laura*—the classic Otto Preminger film featuring Clifton Webb as an obnoxious critic."

That got some laughter going, but it was mostly of the nervous variety; Rath's outburst had cast a shadow over the previously lighthearted proceedings. The casually dressed guests—ranging in age from late teens to senior citizens, with all stops between represented, baby-boomer Yuppie types perhaps the most predominant—rose slowly from the floor, as if their collective bones ached. Chatter soon filled the air, but the merriment quotient seemed low.

"What do you make of that?" Jill asked, looping her arm in mine again, as we headed out into the hall.

"Kirk Rath's a self-important dope," I shrugged. "That's hardly a news flash."

We headed down a hall toward our room and, soon, up ahead, there was Curt, who was standing talking with an attractive brunette about thirty or so, her nice shape snug in a navy blue blazer and gray skirt that seemed to say "hotel management," not guest.

It was an animated conversation, which carried. Curt was shrugging, smiling, doing a lot of body movement in an apparent effort to be charming as well as apologetic. The woman was frowning, shaking her head, not quite buying it. But she seemed more worried than cross.

"I just don't like seeing our Mystery Weekend begin with the murder victim refusing to cooperate," she said.

"I think he's been very cooperative," Curt said. "Everybody in the hotel wants to kill him."

"I don't find this amusing, Mr. Clark."

"Curt. Please. Curt."

"Curt. But our guests pay a premium price for a fun-filled weekend. Your corpse might be better behaved."

Jill and I had caught up with them now.

"Kirk Rath doesn't take dying lying down," Curt was saying, then noticed us: "Oh, Mal—Jill." Curt gestured to the brunette. She was wholesomely pretty; her face was rather full and her eyes were dark brown. Unlike some career women, she took it easy on the makeup. Maybe she was a Quaker.

"This is Mary Wright," he said. "She's the social director here at Mohonk, my boss . . . for the weekend anyway. This is Jill Forrest, Mary. And this is—"

"Mallory," she said. She smiled at both of us, but

extended her hand only to me. "No introduction necessary. You look just like your dustjacket photo."

Jill said, "I think he looks more like his driver's license photo."

Mary Wright ignored that, continuing to hold my hand, saying to me, "I try to read something by all our guest authors. I enjoyed the book I read of yours very much." She still held my hand; hers was warm, mine was sweaty.

Jill seemed less than thrilled that Mary and I were hitting it off so handily, and said to Curt, "Is that little creep really gone?"

"Rath? Yes, I'm afraid so. Thought I might head him off at the pass before he lammed out of here, but no luck. He must've intended doing this all along: he hadn't even checked into his room. He walked directly outside from the Lake Lounge, climbed in his car and drove down the mountain."

Mary finally released my hand, and made a frustrated face. "I'm afraid Curt is right. Our bell captain saw him go."

"What now?" I asked. "Can you stage one of these things without a corpse?"

"Sure," Curt said, waving it off. "Piece of cake. Rath's participation this weekend was minimal, anyway . . . just a gimmick, really."

I nodded slowly. "You mean, having the murder victim be the critic every mystery writer would most like to kill."

"Right. All that was required of Rath was to pose briefly as a bloody corpse tomorrow morning. That and give a lecture and question-and-answer session tomorrow afternoon, after yours. We'll have to fill in there, of course, but we'll come up with something. Rath'll just have to die off-stage."

"We can proceed easily without him," Mary Wright

admitted. But she was still troubled: "What bothers me is his obnoxious behavior back there . . . the cold water he's thrown on my guests."

"They'll get over it," I said. "They're here for a good time, and one pompous put-down from the likes of Rath won't keep the wind out of their sails for very long."

"I hope so," Mary said doubtfully. She smiled, prettily, extended a hand again. "Anyway, your concern is appreciated. And it was a pleasure meeting you, finally."

And she was squeezing my hand again. Giving me a look as warm as her grasp.

"Pleasure's mine. Try another one of my books sometime."

"I intend to," she said, letting loose of me slowly, her fingers brushing my palm rather seductively. "Curt, let's go to my office and figure out exactly how we're going to restructure this thing . . ."

And they were off, talking, gesturing as they went.

"She's nice," I said.

" 'It was a pleasure meeting you *finally*,' " Jill said with infinite sarcasm.

"Huh?"

"Come with me, Romeo." She yanked me by the sweaty hand, and we walked down a hallway. It took a jog and we were suddenly at our room. She had the key and was working it in the door.

"You're not mad at me, are you?" I asked.

"What for?" she said.

"Just because I was polite to that girl."

"She's not a girl. She's thirty-five if she's a day."

"So are you."

"You always know just the right thing to say." She opened the door and smiled tightly and gestured for me to go in. I did.

Jill began undressing, and I sat on one of the twin

beds looking at her while she did. When she was down to her wisp of a bra and her sheer panties, she said, "If I hadn't come along on this trip, you'd be cozying up to that little flirt, wouldn't you?"

"Don't be silly."

"Was that a gun in your pocket, or were you just glad to see her?"

"Hey, there wasn't *anything* in my pocket!"

I got out of my clothes. Turned out the lights. Sat back down on the bed.

"You have no right to be jealous," I said. "You're the one who's leaving *me*, after all."

"I have to. My job in Port City is finished."

"A girl's gotta do what a girl's gotta do."

"I have to work, Mal."

"There are other jobs. You could find something in Port City, or anyway the surrounding area."

"And you could pack up and come with me. You're a writer—you can work anywhere. Nothing's keeping you in Port City."

We'd had this conversation dozens of times, in minorly varying forms. My next remark would be that I had property in Port City—not only my house, but the farmland my parents had left me, which I had to keep an eye on, and ... well, anyway, that's what I would normally say next. And she had something to say that came after that, but to hell with it. An impasse is an impasse.

"We weren't going to talk about this," I said, "this trip."

"I know."

"So how did we get onto it?"

Her voice was a little sad as she said, "I guess I can't stand the thought of, after I leave, you taking up with some little chippy the minute I'm out of the city limits."

"Chippy?" I said, savoring the word. "Chippy? I was

thinking more of finding some floozie. Or perhaps a hussy. Or maybe a bimbo; yeah, that's the ticket. I think I'll find me a bimbo to take your place, the minute you leave town."

"Very funny," she said, and there was enough moonlight filtering in through the window for me to see that she was indeed smiling a little.

"What do you want to do about these twin beds?" I asked.

"Push them together," she said.

"Good idea."

I moved the nightstand out of the way, and we mated twin beds, and then we just plain mated.

"We should have made a fire," she said, snuggling with me in my twin bed.

"What do you call what we just did?"

"You know what I mean. It'd be very romantic, the fireplace going in this otherwise dark room."

" 'Otherwise dark room,' huh? Pretty fancy talk. You must hang around with a writer or something."

She snuggled closer. "An author," she said.

"We'll have our fire tomorrow night. Forecast says it's going to get colder and maybe snow some, over the weekend."

"An author who talks like a TV weatherman," Jill amended, then sat up in bed and stretched; the moonlight made her body look smooth, bathed it in ivory.

"I'm going to take a shower," she said, yawning.

"Do you want to get dressed and take in Pete's movie, after?"

"I don't think so. I've seen *Laura* a million times. Anyway, I'm bushed. You can go if you like, though."

"You'd trust me?"

"For the next couple hours or so. Your powers of recuperation being what they are."

"You couldn't have trusted me that long when I was twenty-five."

"Well, Mal, you're thirty-five, like the rest of us, and I'll trust you till midnight."

She slid out of bed and padded barefoot into the bathroom and the sound of the shower's spray soon began lulling me. I lay there trying to decide whether I wanted to get out of bed and get dressed and take in that flick. I was fairly keyed up, despite the long day. But the sheets felt cool and the blankets warm and the bed soft and the phone woke me.

It was only a minute or so later; the shower was still doing its rain dance. But the phone, over on the table by the window, was ringing.

I sat up, yawned, tasted my mouth (which in one minute had accumulated the unpleasant film and sour breath of a full night's sleep) and bumped into things as I made my clumsy way across the room to the insistent phone.

"Yes," I said.

"Mal? Curt. I hope I didn't wake you—it's early yet, I didn't expect you to sack out so soon."

"Me, either." He sounded a little hyper. "What's up?"

"I wondered if you'd mind doing double duty tomorrow."

"How so?"

"You have a speech to give, but after that, we need to fill Rath's slot with something, remember?"

"Yeah . . ."

"I was hoping you and Tom and Jack could throw together a sort of panel on the resurgence of the hardboiled private-eye in mystery fiction."

"That's a mouthful, Curt . . . but, sure. Why not?"

"I knew you'd come through for me."

"You sound a little frazzled."

"Mary Wright's upset with me. She's an efficient

young woman, but she doesn't deal well with surprises, or with changes of plan. She doesn't know how to think on her feet, like us mystery writers."

"I do most of my thinking sitting down, but I know what you mean."

"Anyway, I promised her I'd get everything rescheduled tonight. That way she can sleep soundly, I guess."

"Well, anything I can do to help out."

"Much appreciated, Mal. I guess I screwed up, thinking I could depend on that pompous ass Rath to play my corpse."

"The only thing you can depend on that pompous ass to be," I said, "is a pompous ass."

"You're right," he said, laughing a little. Then he sighed. "This thing is starting to get to me. I just hope we don't get snowbound."

"Why, is that what they're predicting now?"

"Yeah. Heavy snow tonight or tomorrow. Is it snowing out there?"

I glanced out the window. It wasn't snowing; there was nothing out there, except two people standing on that open walkway bridge, in the gazebo. They seemed to be arguing.

"No snow," I said.

"Yet," he said fatalistically.

We hung up, and I stood there a moment looking out at the moonlit lake and cliffs and evergreens.

But those people in the gazebo got in the way of any peacefully reflective moment.

The two figures were both heavily bundled in dark winter clothing, one of them, at left, a stocky figure in a red and black ski mask—probably, but not necessarily, a man. The other, at right, was bareheaded and obviously a man, or one very short-haired woman. Two figures standing on the gazebo at night was hardly remarkable, even if they were arguing—except these figures were going beyond that, shoving each other around. The bareheaded guy gave Ski Mask a shove that about knocked him (or her) off the bridge—a fall of about a story and a half.

Ski Mask managed to keep his/her balance, and the shoving stopped, but the body English of the two figures was even more disturbing. They were, indeed, arguing. Violently. Their gestures, at least, were violent.

It wasn't my business, but I couldn't not watch; and I felt oddly removed from it—distant—as if I were the audience and they were the play, an ominous pantomime, as the thick pane of glass that separated me from the outside was keeping the sound of the argument from getting in. I couldn't hear them argue, but I could watch them. Which I did, my face tensed, my eyes narrowed, watched the quarrel turn into something ugly.

Something dangerous.

The bareheaded man pushed past Ski Mask and walked down off the bridge, onto the patch of ground sloping down to the lake, which stretched out before my window; his feet scuffed the powdery snow.

Ski Mask followed quickly, down off the bridge, sending up little flurries as his/her feet cut a quick path toward the bareheaded man, who didn't seem to know his pursuer was behind him. Something caught in my throat as I saw an object in Ski Mask's hand catch the moonlight and wink.

A blade.

Ski Mask's free hand settled on the near shoulder of the bareheaded man—they were less than a hundred feet from my window, now—and spun him around. I cried out, but couldn't be heard, it seemed; my role was so minor in this little drama as to be meaningless. The bareheaded man's back was to me now, as Ski Mask raised his/her arm, the blade catching the moonlight again and I yelled, "Hey! Goddammit, stop!," my mouth almost against the window, fogging it up, and I rubbed my fist against the fog and cleared it and could see that knife going up, coming down, going up, coming down, stabbing, slashing, stabbing, slashing.

The bareheaded man stumbled toward me; he was scarcely fifty feet from me when he fell, his face distorted from two long ragged red strokes from the blade, his dark blue quilted winter jacket shredded in front, turning wet with blood. Then he dropped into the snow, face down, and Ski Mask began hauling him away by the ankles.

I was trying to open the window now, but it was jammed, and I was yelling, screaming, they hadn't even fucking seen me, and Jill hadn't heard me either, the needles of the shower in her ears and I ran into the bathroom, pulled her out, confused, naked, and wet.

"Mal, what the hell?"

"Look out there!"

"I'm naked, for God's sake—I don't want to stand next to a window."

I pulled a blanket off the bed and tossed it at her.

"Now, look, dammit! What do you see?"

"Nothing," she said.

I looked out the window.

I didn't see anything, either.

Just the lake, the gazebo and bridge, the cliffs, the evergreens, the snowy ground, as peaceful and unreal as a landscape painting you'd buy in a shopping mall. You could see where some feet had disturbed the snow, but that was the only sign.

The body was gone. From the window, at least, there was no blood in the snow.

And certainly no body.

Even if I had clearly seen through my window the blood-streaked face of a dying Kirk S. Rath.

6

...

"I don't know what the hell to do," I said, although I was in fact in the process of doing something: throwing on some clothes.

Jill was drying off with a towel, looking at me carefully, as if I were a UFO she wasn't sure she was seeing.

"You're sure you saw what you said you saw," she said flatly, a statement.

"No, I'm not sure. It might have been Santa and his reindeer, or Charo's midnight show at the Sands. But it sure looked like somebody getting murdered to me."

"Calm down," she said, coming over to me, naked, which is no way to calm me down. She patted my shoulder, smiled reassuringly, like I was her child who'd had a bad dream.

"I'm calm," I said. "I am not having an acid flashback, either. Haight Ashbury was a long time ago."

She tried a kidding smile. "Maybe you're going into television withdrawal."

"Yeah, right. I haven't seen any mindless violence all day, so my psyche conjures some up for me. Well, my imagination rates an Emmy tonight. Jill, I'm shaking. Excuse me."

I brushed past her and kneeled before the porcelain god and made that offering sometimes known as a technicolor yawn. Soon she was kneeling beside me, dressed now, putting an arm around me, patting me.

"You'll be okay, sugar," she said.

I stood up on my rubbery legs. "Try to avoid calling me any pet names that are in any way related to any of the major food groups, okay? For the next hour or so, at least."

"Anything you say, dumplin'," she said, with her ironic smile, rising, and I told her she was a caution.

Then I was heading out into the hall and she was following.

"Where are you going?" she said.

"Curt's just down the hall ... I got to talk to him."

"Maybe you should call the front desk. Call the cops."

I shook my head. "I'll talk to Curt, first. He'll know what to do."

I knocked and almost immediately the door cracked open and Curt peeked out; the sliver of him visible told me he was in his underwear.

"Now you've got *me* out of bed," he said, with a wry one-sided grin. "So we're even. What's up?"

"I'm not sure."

His face turned serious. "Is something wrong, Mal? Really wrong?"

"I think I just witnessed a murder."

He pulled his head back and pursed his lips and narrowed his eyes in an expression that said, Are you putting me on?

"I am not putting you on. I just saw something, and it looked a hell of a lot like a man getting killed."

"You really *are* serious. . . ."

"I really am."

His expression grave now, he said, "Give me a second. Kim's already in bed; I'll just wake her and let her know I'm stepping out for a second."

The door closed. I heard him say something to Kim in there, and a minute or so later he emerged fully dressed, in the same patched-elbow sports coat and cords as before.

"Let's go to your room," he said.

"Good idea. That's where I saw it from."

Jill and I led him there, where I took him to the window and pointed out at the now peaceful white landscape that had minutes before seemed violent and blood-red. I explained what I'd seen.

As my explanation progressed, a sly smile began to form on Curt's face; by the conclusion, he stood with his arms folded, rocking on his heels, looking down at me—both figuratively and literally—with open amusement.

"I fail to see what's even remotely comic about this," I said, petulantly. Curt was one of my literary godfathers, and I didn't like feeling a fool before him.

"They reeled you in, Mal," he said, chuckling. I hate it when people chuckle.

"What the hell do you mean?"

He chortled. I hate it even more when they chortle. "These Mystery Weekenders have obviously staged a Grand Guignol farce for your benefit."

"What? You got to be kidding!"

"Not at all. Not in the least. You've never been to the Mystery Weekend here at the illustrous Mohonk Mountain House. You don't *know* what sort of shenanigans to expect."

"Shenanigans. Since when is slashing a guy to ribbons a *shenanigan*?"

"When it's staged by some overly ambitious game-players."

Jill was standing off to one side, but now she moved in between Curt and me, like a mediator.

"You're saying this was a practical joke," she said, "played by some of the Mystery Weekenders."

"Exactly," he said. "Kirk Rath stormed out of here, insulting the intelligence of the players, refusing to co-operate. Leaving before the fun could begin."

"That's right," I said.

"So isn't it natural that some of the players might want to stage what he denied them? Namely, his 'murder'?"

I let out a sigh of exasperation. "And just how exactly did they convince Rath to stick around and go along with this farce?"

"They didn't."

"I saw Kirk Rath die!"

"Did you? How close was he to your window?"

I thought about it. "Well, not all that close—not all that far, either."

"Could it have been someone else?"

"I don't think so. . . ."

"Possibly someone who looked something like Rath—similar hair, similar build."

"Maybe," I granted.

"And you had Rath on the brain—you had the 'murder' of Rath on the brain, specifically. If someone who resembled him were 'killed' outside your window, wouldn't Rath come immediately to mind?"

"Curt, I don't think so. . . ."

He was shaking his head now, gesturing out the window at the now barren stage where I'd witnessed what he insisted was a performance.

"You haven't been here before," Curt said. "You don't know the lengths these lovable crazies will go to. When we assemble on Sunday morning, for the teams to present their solutions to my mystery, their presentations will be as elaborate as an off-Broadway play. And not far off Broadway at that."

Jill looked at Curt thoughtfully and said, "You give an award for the team presenting their solution in the most creative manner, don't you? Whether they solve the mystery correctly or not."

"That's exactly right," Curt said.

"Don't encourage him," I told Jill sternly; she gave me an apologetic look and shrugged, but I could see she was being swayed by this. "You didn't see what *I* saw," I reminded her.

"She didn't?" Curt said.

"No. She was in the shower."

"Cleanliness is next to godliness," Curt shrugged.

"Why are you trivializing this?"

He put a fatherly hand on my shoulder. "I don't mean to. I just know the foolishness that goes on here. Jill is right about the award for most creative presentation. Toward that end, many of the players bring along theatrical gear—make-up, fake blood, the works. A number of them are theater professionals. If they noticed somebody here who resembled Rath, and could convince him to play along, with a little expert makeup, they could, at a distance, *fool* somebody . . . like you. Not me. Because I'm a veteran of this cheerful nonsense."

Cheerful nonsense.

"So," I said, "I'm the butt of a fraternity initiation sort of joke, then?"

He waved that off. "Not you specifically. It could have just as easily been me that witnessed this 'murder.'"

The guests know that the authors are all grouped together in this wing of the hotel. Do you think it's an accident that this event was staged outside all our windows? You just happened to be the one of us who caught the show."

"And the hook," I said.

"And the hook," he said, nodding. He slid an arm around my shoulder and walked me away from the window. Jill followed. "Mal, I'm convinced you've witnessed a prank, nothing more—a grisly piece of impromptu theater by some Mystery Weekenders unknown."

"*I'm* not convinced," I said.

He walked out into the hall and I followed him. So did Jill.

"Well," he said, "we can go down to the front desk and report it. Right now. New Paltz is nearby; the police could come right up."

"Let's do that."

"I wish you wouldn't. Let me tell you why."

"Please do."

He gestured with an open palm, in a reasoning manner. "If the police come up here, you're going to get some of the hotel's guests in trouble, and some very bad publicity could be stirred up. You might put a damper on the whole weekend; Kirk Rath's little temper tantrum would be nothing compared to this. I don't think that would be a useful thing, do you?"

"I . . . suppose not."

"Besides which, everybody here saw Rath leave in a huff. In a minute and a huff. How could he be who you saw out your window? He *left*." Curt hunched his shoulders and gestured with both hands in mock seriousness; very melodramatic, he intoned, "Or did he come back? If so, why? In which case, what was he *doing* here, then?"

"I don't know," I admitted, ignoring his kidding manner. "But those strike me as legitimate questions."

"You strike me as somebody who's had a long day and ought to catch some z's."

"I'm tired, but I'm not seeing things."

"I know you aren't," he said, unconvincingly. "Hey. Why don't you go have a look around outside? If you find anything, see anything, come knock on my door. I'll be up for another hour—I'm working on some last minute materials for tomorrow's fun and games. We have to kill Rath again tomorrow morning, you know— *in absentia.* Anyway, if after that you still want to go down to the desk, I'll accompany you."

"All right," I said.

He smiled and patted my shoulder again. "But if you don't find anything, then go get some sleep. These gameplayers are crafty and they're cute—don't let 'em get to you. You'll need to be fresh in the morning. You have to play one of my suspects, remember."

Then he shut himself back in his room.

I looked at Jill.

"Could he be right about this?" she said.

"Yeah," I said.

"But do you think he's right?"

"No. But *he* thinks he's right. And I can see how this looks to him."

"Yes."

"Only he didn't see what I saw out that window, did he?"

"No."

"Let's get our coats."

"Let's," she said.

I stopped at the front desk and asked if I could borrow a flashlight; the guy behind the counter was accommodating and friendly—he didn't even ask what I wanted it for, he just handed it to me. I wondered how accommodating (and friendly) he'd be if I came back later and reported a murder. Not to mention a disappearing corpse.

And it had disappeared, all right. The snow on the ground outside my window showed footprints, and you could see where something had been dragged away—but only for a few feet. Then the footprints resumed; only the wind was blowing the snow around and to call these footprints, in the sense that some real detective could pour plaster of Paris into them and make a moulage and trap a suspect, would be a joke. You could tell somebody had been walking in the snow, and that was all. That was the most you could say.

And there was no sign of blood. Or theatrical makeup or ketchup either.

I poked around with the flashlight, looking in the trees and bushes, Jill at my side. Nothing. We walked up on the bridge; stood in the gazebo; looked out at the impassive frozen lake and the mountain beyond. The night was chilly, and the wind had teeth. So did we, and they were chattering.

We went inside.

We went to bed.

"Some detective," I said.

She was cuddling me on my side of the pushed-together twins.

"Who says you're a detective? You're a writer."

"I've played at detective before. You helped me once, remember?"

"I vaguely remember."

That was sarcasm: the time she'd helped me out, she had seen the aftermath of some very serious violence; I'd almost been killed, and two other men had. So she knew that none of this was anything I was taking lightly. She also knew I'd had some experience with crime, with violence, and wouldn't be easily fooled by pranksters.

"Want to go down to the front desk?" she asked.

"And report what I saw?"

"Yeah."

"I don't know what I saw anymore."

"Could it have been staged, like Curt thinks?"

"It did seem sort of . . . 'Staged' isn't the word exactly. But it was like I was watching a scene in a movie, not real life."

"Don't discount its reality for that reason. I was in a rather bad accident once; I wasn't hurt badly, but the car I was in got hit head on by a drunk driver."

"Jesus. I never heard this story."

She was sitting up in bed, now. "Well, this guy and I were driving home late at night, and a drunk driver got hypnotized by our lights or something and kept coming right at us. He wasn't going fast, really, and we were able to slow almost to a stop, by the time he hit us. We swerved and he crashed into the side of the car. The guy I was with broke his arm; I had a little whiplash, is all."

"That's a relatively happy ending, then. But what's your point?"

"My point is this: I had a minute at least during which to watch that car come toward us. Knowing the accident was going to happen. Knowing I might be killed."

"Did you panic?"

"No. That's the strange part. I felt detached. The world went slow motion on me. And—as you said—it was like watching a scene in a movie."

"Then you think I may really have witnessed a murder."

"I think you may have. What do you think?"

"I think maybe Curt's right. Maybe it *was* a prank."

"Yeah?"

"And maybe it wasn't."

She smiled, sighed. "We better try to get some sleep. You do have a role to play tomorrow morning."

She was right; I was, after all, one of the prime suspects in Curt's whodunit. I didn't know what was going on in *that* mystery, either—all I knew for sure was that I wasn't the killer.

But neither one of us could get to sleep till I got up and shut the curtain over that damn window.

PART TWO

...

Friday

7

. . .

Jill was showering again. The sound of it brought me up out of a deep but turbulent sleep. Closing the curtain on that window last night hadn't kept the images I'd viewed out of it from returning to mock me in almost delirious Daliesque dreams—none of which were sticking with me, exactly, as I sat up and rubbed the sand out of my eyes. But the feel of them lingered, the mood, and I knew they'd been about what I'd seen from my ringside seat at the window. I did remember one specific dream fragment: crashing through the window, glass shattering but harmlessly, I leapt like a hero into the fray, yanking the ski mask off the killer's head . . . and seeing the face of a stranger.

When Jill came out, her slim dark body barely wrapped in a towel, another smaller one on her head like a turban, she looked like a cute Arab. I told her so.

"Oh?" she said. "And you look like hell."

"Sweet talker."

"Rough night?"

"Awful. Sick dreams. I don't have to tell you what about."

She sat next to me on the bed. "Does it seem any less real today?"

I hadn't been up long, but, groggy or not, I was firm on this one. "No," I said. "What I saw was convincing."

"What do you want to do about it?"

"I'm not sure. I'll think in the shower."

I did; the water invigorated me, first cold, then hot, and some notions started tickling the inside of my skull and I started to smile. I'd been tired last night; beaten down by agents and editors and bus rides and, just possibly, Mohonk Mystery Weekenders. Screwy dreams or not, I'd had some sleep, and this was a new day. Something would be done about what I'd witnessed.

I started to sing.

When I came out in my Tarzan towel, Jill was dressed—a red jacket over a white blouse with navy slacks, patriotism Kamali style—and she smiled on one side of her pretty face and said, "You're the only person I know of who sings 'Splish Splash, I was takin' a bath' in the shower."

"World's number one Bobby Darin fan," I explained without embarrassment and a little pride. "If you want something more current, go out with somebody ten years younger. Than either of us."

"I better not risk it," she said, sitting at a dresser before a mirror, putting on some abstract-shape earrings. "Heavy Metal in the shower might get me electrocuted."

I was over at the phone, by the curtained window, dialing. "You haven't even met this younger guy yet," I said, "and already you're in the shower with him. Have you no shame?"

"Who are you calling?"

"Front desk. Want to check up on something."

"Front desk," a female said. A nice sultry alto.

"This is Mr. Mallory in room sixty-four. I'm one of the guest authors this weekend."

"Yes, Mr. Mallory." Perky for an alto.

"I wonder if you could give me some information about the hotel?"

"We're always anxious to provide information about the mountain *house*, Mr. Mallory."

The staff got touchy here when you referred to Mohonk as a "hotel."

"When my bus arrived last night," I said, "a man was on duty down toward the bottom of the mountain. In a sort of a little house."

"Yes. That's the Gate House."

"I didn't see a gate."

"There was one years ago. It's still called the Gate House. We're big on tradition at Mohonk, Mr. Mallory."

"Oh. Okay. Well, the bus driver checked in with him before we headed up the mountain."

"Yes."

"Is that common procedure?"

"Absolutely, Mr. Mallory. No one is allowed in unless their name is on the list."

"I see. You don't get a lot of walk-in traffic at the hotel, then?"

"None. And it's a house."

"Right. How long is that guard on duty?"

"Well, there are several shifts. But someone is there all the time."

"Someone's on duty twenty-four hours?"

"That's right."

"Any way up to the hotel other than that road?"

"It's a house, sir. And no there isn't."

"Any way to get to that road, bypassing the Gate House?"

"No."

"Hmmm. I wonder if I could talk to the man who was on duty in the Gate House last evening."

"Sir, I believe he'd be sleeping, now . . . and I couldn't give out his home number. You might check with someone in management."

"Okay. Thank you very much. You run a nice hotel here."

"It's a house," she said, but there was a smile in her voice; she knew I was needling her.

Jill was putting on her lipstick. "What was that about?"

I slipped on my clothes and as I did told her what the front desk alto had told me.

"So if Rath *really* left," she said, pointing at me like a teacher, "he'd probably have been seen by the guard at the Gate House."

"Right. And more important—if he left only to *return*, he'd have been *seen* returning. Not only seen, he'd have had to log in with the guard."

"You mean you'd have a specific time."

"Exactly." I was smiling. Also dialing.

"*Now* who are you calling?"

"Kirk Rath," I said.

The cornflower-blue eyes got very large, and she sat on the edge of the bed nearby. I called the hotel (mountain house) operator and she put me through to information for Albany, New York; Rath's home number was listed. I wasn't sure it would be. On the other hand, somebody as adversary by nature as Rath wouldn't duck a fight by going through life unlisted.

The phone rang in my ear. I pulled the curtain as I waited. The view out the window seemed even less real in the cold gray dawn; several couples in winter clothes were making their way across the little bridge. One couple paused in the gazebo, to chat, their breath smoking.

I didn't find it particularly inviting—winter not being my favorite season in any state, New York and Iowa included—but neither was it ominous.

On the ninth ring, he answered: "This is Kirk Rath."

"Kirk!" I said. "This is—"

"At the sound of the tone, leave any message you might have for me, obscene or otherwise."

Shit.

At the tone I said, "Kirk, this is Mallory up at Mohonk. If you're alive, give me a call today, as soon as possible."

I hung up. Scratched my head.

"Think he'll call back?" she said.

"That hinges at least partly on whether or not he's alive," I said, sitting by her.

"Do you think he might be home and just has the answer machine on?"

"With answer machines, that's always a possibility. It's still relatively early—he could be sleeping. A little later this morning I can call the business number."

"Didn't you say the *Chronicler* was published out of his house?"

"Yup," I said. "Everything but printed on the premises. But it's a separate number, the business is, and I'll bet his staff will be working there even if he's not. They live right there. It's like a big fraternity house, I understand."

"So you can find out from *somebody* whether he showed up or not."

"Should be able to."

Jill sighed. "It's too bad Rath himself didn't just answer and put an end to this."

I said, "Suppose last night he had second thoughts, and came back, to play his weekend role? And got killed—*really* killed—for his trouble."

"Who *by*?"

"Jesus, Jill. I haven't even been able to establish the poor S.O.B. is really dead. Don't ask me to name the killer just yet, okay?"

"Okay," she said, with a little smile.

"But one thing I do intend to find out," I said, standing, looking down at her, touching her nose with the tip of a forefinger, "is which of these teams of game-players has theater pros on 'em, and who among 'em brought their makeup kits along."

She stood and straightened the collar on my pullover shirt, the type the Beach Boys and I have been wearing for decades.

"Feeling more like a detective now, are you?" she said.

"Thinking like one. That long day yesterday threw me."

She gave me a peck of a kiss and a wry grin and said, "Put on your 'Miami Vice' jacket and let's go down and have breakfast."

"Did you have to mention 'Miami Vice'? This is Friday and we still don't have a TV."

"I asked at the desk about that," she said, helping me into my white linen jacket. "They have a projection TV in one of the parlors."

"But will it fit in this room?"

I opened the door for her and in the hall we met Jack Flint and his wife, Janis, just coming back from breakfast apparently. Jack wore a lime blazer and a pastel green shirt, and Janis another floral print dress, yellows and greens; they looked like California. I wondered if, God help me, I looked like Iowa.

We exchanged good mornings and, with a small wicked grin, Jack said, "I hear you got stung last night."

"Pardon?"

"Curt mentioned that some of the game-players staged a little skit outside your window."

"So it seems," I said. "I think George Romero directed it."

Janis cocked her head like she hadn't heard me right, not understanding the reference; movie buff Jill said to her, "*Night of the Living Dead.*"

"Oh," Janis said. Nice of Jill to coach the wife of a screenwriter in film lore.

Meanwhile, Jack was laughing. "Bunch of overgrown kids. We'll be putting on a show for *them*, in an hour or so."

He meant, of course, Curt's mystery in which we were playing roles.

"Yes," Janis said, "and I'm scared to death."

Jill resisted telling her that that was the title of Bela Lugosi's only color film and said instead, "Why? Are you playing one of the suspects?"

"Yes, I'm afraid so," Janis said, with a nervous little smile. "Aren't you?"

"No. Mal didn't tell them I was coming along till the last minute."

Janis grasped Jill's arm, in mock panic that was only part mock. "You wouldn't want to take over *my* role, would you?"

Jill grinned and shook her head no. "I'm no mystery fan, or puzzle freak, either. I'm here for a little peace and quiet; I mean to roam these endless halls and sit in every one of the hundred and eighty-one gazebos on this property. As Elmer Fudd once said, 'West and wewaxsation at wast.' "

I put a hand on Jack's arm and said in almost a whisper, "Did you see any of that out your window last night?"

"Your little passion play? No. When did it go on?"

"Just before eleven."

"Janis and I went up and watched Pete's flick. I'd forgotten how good *Laura* was."

"Yeah," I said, glumly, "well, my favorite Otto Preminger film is *Skidoo*."

Jack did a little take; he'd apparently seen *Skidoo*.

"He's kidding," Jill said, and took me by the arm and we exchanged good-byes with the Flints and were off to breakfast.

Where, in the big pine dining hall, we found Tom Sardini sitting at our designated table, having a cup of coffee; Cynthia Crystal and Tim Culver were over at Curt's table, only neither Curt nor wife Kim were present. I said good morning to Cynthia and Tim, both of whom (even the normally dour Culver) grinned at me. I had the feeling I was a comical figure.

Jill went on over to our table, but I stopped and stood behind and between Cynthia and Culver, and leaned in, a hand on the back of either of their chairs.

"Good morning, gang," I said. "What's so funny?"

"Oh, Mal," Cynthia said, the arcs of her pale blonde hair swinging as she looked back at me, blue eyes sparkling, "I just *treasure* it when you behave like a gullible hick."

"Me, too," I said. "Takes me back to the days when I traveled with Spike Jones and the band."

Culver's smile was gone now; he sensed my feathers were ruffled. So did Cynthia—she just didn't care. But Culver said: "Curt told us about that practical joke. Didn't mean to rub it in."

"Oh, Mal," Cynthia said, "how could you fall for amateur theatrics like that?"

"Why?" I said, looking at her sharply. "Did you see it too?"

"No, no," Cynthia said, brushing the notion away with one lovely hand. "Last evening Tim and I went walking for hours around this charming old hotel."

"House," I corrected.

"Whatever," Cynthia said. "But I've done several of these weekends before—never Mohonk, but Tim and I were on an ocean cruise variation of this, for Karen and Billy Palmer, last year. We know all about the lengths these lovable loons will go to, to get in the spirit of mystery and crime and spillikins in the parlor."

At Mohonk, that could be a lot of spillikins, because there were a lot of parlors.

I said, "Your room does look out on the lake, though."

"Yes," Cynthia said. "And it's a lovely view."

"That's debatable," I said.

She pressed my arm. "You're such a child. That's what I love about you."

"Yeah," I said. "I figure immaturity is one of my more admirable qualities. That, and poor judgment."

Culver said, "You don't seriously think you saw anything more than some amateur theatrics, do you?"

"I guess not," I said.

Cynthia's brittle laugh rose to the high ceiling. "If only it were true."

"Pardon?" I said.

She was putting preserves on a muffin as she responded: "If only somebody *had* knifed that little bastard."

I had no answer for that, so I smiled and nodded and joined Jill.

"So," Tom said as I sat across from him, "somebody made a sap out of you."

A waiter poured coffee in my cup and I drank some. "It's nice of Curt to tell everybody what a fool I made of myself last night."

Tom smiled; even his beard twinkled. "So they murdered ol' Kirk Rath in the moonlight, huh?"

"That's what it looked like."

"I tell ya," Tom said, "this place is like some kind of demented summer camp. I mean, they really go all out here."

"No kidding."

I wrote up our order on the little menu sheet provided for us—French toast for me, scrambled eggs for Jill—and Tom sat appraising me over his coffee cup.

"What is it, Mal?" he said.

"What's what?"

"Come on. I've known you for a long time. Nobody likes a joke better than you. But you're bristling about this thing."

"I was in a great mood till I walked in here and realized I was wearing size eighteen shoes."

Jill seemed uneasy; I think she was hoping I'd leave this alone. And I would have, but Tom pressed on: "I still say you like a good laugh. But you're not laughing. Why?"

I smiled at him, a poker player's smile. "What would you say if I told you I'm not convinced what I saw wasn't real?"

His expression turned blank. "You think somebody killed Kirk Rath outside your window. Really *killed* him?"

I shrugged. Sipped my coffee.

"Aw, Mal, that's crazy."

"If murder never happened, Tom, we'd be in another line of work."

He gestured with two hands; be reasonable. "But Rath left," he said.

"Supposedly. Where's your room?"

"What?"

"Your room. We're in number sixty-four. What room are you in?"

"Just up the hall from you—fifty-eight."

"Do you have a view of the lake from your room? The gazebo, the little Japanese bridge?"

"Sure."

"Did you see anything last night? Around ten-thirty?"

"Just Pete's movie."

"Did you see Jack Flint there?"

"He was sitting a few rows behind me. Why? What is this, 'Dragnet'?"

Jill said, "Don't mention TV shows to him, Tom. He's still suffering video withdrawal."

Jill was trying to lighten the mood, but it wasn't necessary; Tom wasn't offended—he was just curious, interested.

"You really think Rath was murdered," he said.

"It's a possibility, that's all."

"And I'm a suspect!" He said this with glee.

"He suspects everyone," Jill said, "and he suspects no one."

Now I was a little embarrassed. Just a little.

"Look," I said, "I just want to know if I'm the only guy who saw this particular 'Saturday Night Live' sketch."

"TV reference again," Jill said. "Watch it."

"Maybe it was staged specifically *for* you," Tom said.

"Curt didn't think so," I said. "Everybody knows all the guest authors are billeted in that wing. Curt says I just happened to be the one who got snookered."

Tom pushed his empty coffee cup aside. "What do *you* think?"

"I think I'm going to do what all these game-players are doing this weekend."

"What's that?"

Dum da dum dum.

"Play detective."

8

• • •

You are Lester Denton—age thirty-seven. Small town boy, introverted, Middletown High Class of '67—Least Likely to Succeed (also member of Chess and Poetry Clubs). A life-long nerd, you are an asexual bachelor living with your rather wealthy, widowed mother. Despite being a timid soul who rarely ventures out of the house, you have succeeded in realizing a life-long dream: you have had a mystery novel published, *The Apple Red Take-Off*. But your dreams have been dashed by critic Roark K. Sloth, in whose *Mystery Carbuncle* your debut novel has been unmercifully panned. You blame the lack of financial success of the novel directly on Sloth's heartless review. When you check into the Mohawk Mountain House one wintry Thursday evening for a mystery writer's convention, you are at first distressed to find Sloth one of the guest lecturers. Then, upon second thought, you decide his presence presents a unique opportunity to rectify an unpleasant situation. You go to Sloth's room that evening and offer the critic money to "simply ignore" the next (and, if sales don't pick up, probably last) Lester Denton novel, *Death Is a Fatal Disease*. Sloth not only laughs at you, he pledges to reveal your "pathetic" attempt to bribe him in a *Carbuncle* article; and when, though flustered, you shrewdly point out that there are no witnesses to the bribery attempt, and therefore Sloth would be putting himself on the line for a libel suit, the critic laughs smugly and reveals a pocket tape recorder—on which the entire conversation has been captured! You leave, tail tucked between your legs, defeated, but notice private-eye Rob Darsini coming down the hall, apparently on his way to Sloth's room. The next morning, you are as surprised as the other guests to discover that Sloth has been found dead in his hotel room with a knife in his back, slumped over his typewriter, a sheet in which bears the cryptic dying clue: TOVL FOF OY. And no tape of your bribe attempt is found.

YOU WILL NOT LIE—but you will not volunteer information about the visit to Sloth's room unless asked by an interrogator. You will, if confronted directly, admit having attempted to bribe Sloth. You will

> reveal having seen Darsini. You are not
> the killer; you did not steal the tape.

This, as written by Curt Clark, was all I knew about the character I would be portraying in the Mohonk mystery this weekend; each of the author guests had received similar instruction sheets by mail, though we weren't privy to each other's. I tucked mine back in the envelope it had come in (MALLORY—EYES ONLY), which also included a sheet with one-paragraph descriptions of the other suspects, and placed it in my inside suitcoat pocket, for handy reference. I looked at myself in the mirror, straightened my red bow tie, which was color-coordinated with my pale pink shirt, combed back my heavily Brylcreamed hair, which was parted in the middle, adjusted my window-glass glasses so that they were halfway down the bridge of my nose, under which a pencil-line moustache twitched, and adjusted the SUSPECT badge on one lapel of my double-breasted black-and-red-and-white plaid corduroy suit.

I was, for all intents and purposes, Lester Denton, suspect in the Roark K. Sloth murder, *The Case of the Curious Critic*. While I'd never thought of myself as a nerd, nor did I have a wealthy, widowed mother, Denton was, in some respects, a cute if nasty-around-the-edges parody of myself and my own situation with Kirk Rath. In light of the murder I'd witnessed (or was that "murder"?), I found the wry, sardonic echoes of real life in Curt's scenario more disturbing than amusing. I wondered if the other authors were playing roles that struck them as somewhat uncomfortably similar to themselves and their own bitterness toward Rath.

"You make a truly convincing nerd," Jill said, smirking cutely, skin crinkling around the corners of her cornflower-blue eyes.

"I know you are," I said nasally, "but what am I?"

"Takes one to know one," she said nasally back at me.

I gave her a sloppy, nerdy smooch and slipped my arm around her shoulder and we walked out into the hall and down to Curt's room, where all the role-playing authors were assembling, prior to the first of the weekend's two interrogation sessions, which was to begin just fifteen minutes from now. Partylike sounds were going on behind Curt's door; we paused before going in.

"You look so cute with that little mustache," she said, pinching my cheek (facial cheek). "I'm tempted to just be a groupie and hang around and watch *your* performance."

I shook my head no. "I'd really prefer you to circulate—listen to the other 'suspects.' "

"What am I supposed to get out of that?"

"I don't know," I admitted. "Just make sure you catch a glimpse of each of them, noting whether or not they seem unduly ill at ease."

"If they do, it won't necessarily mean anything more than stage fright."

"Maybe not, but jot down some notes anyway. Also, look for any particularly obsessive game-players; anybody who seems to be taking this too seriously, or is really pushy in the interrogation sessions."

"How am I supposed to know what their names are?"

I pointed to my badge. "They'll be wearing them."

"Ah."

We knocked on Curt's door, which Curt himself opened. "Well, Lester Denton in the flesh!" he said above the crowd's conversation, doing a pop-eyed take. "Where on earth did you find that suit?"

Jill said, "You'd be surprised. I didn't have to dig all that far back in his closet to unearth it."

I shrugged. "The early seventies were a do-your-own-thing kind of era; apparently my thing was tacky plaid suits."

"Yesterday's trendsetter," Curt said, ushering us in, "today's *nebbish*." His room, which was filled with the other suspects, was easily twice as large as ours, a suite really; the fireplace was bigger, and the twin beds were boxed together, I noted. The suspects were all in costume, of course; only Curt was in civvies, a casual blue shirt and brown slacks. He had a glass of something in his hand—ginger ale, as it turned out—and he got us some.

"Well," he said, "you certainly look your part. Ready to live it as well as look it?"

"Sure. How long did you say this session's going to be?"

"One hour; they get another hour with you tomorrow morning. Say, you know, you really loosened everybody up." He gestured to the costumed suspects around him.

"How's that?"

He raised his eyebrows. "Ah, well . . ." He put them back down. "I think my sense of black comedy got the best of me, in whipping up this mystery; some of the guests—Jack Flint and my brother, in particular—took a little offense at the way I'd written their roles, especially in regard to 'Roark K. Sloth.' "

"Hit a little too close to home, did you?"

He mock-grimaced for just a moment. "Guess so. Anyway, that prank that got pulled on you last night, when the word got around, gave everybody a laugh."

"I noticed."

He put a hand on my shoulder, pretended to be somber. "You're not angry with me?"

"For making me the laughingstock of Mohonk? I'm livid. I'll never speak to you again."

He shrugged, mugged. "Just so we cleared *that* up,"

he said, and moved on to mingle with other members of his cast.

Jill, who'd been at my side listening to all this, said, "You sure cut that guy a lot of slack."

"He's done me plenty of favors. Remember my mentioning that one of my teachers at a writers' conference helped me get an agent?"

"Sure."

"Well, Curt was that writer. I'd written him fan letters for years, and my early short stories were all brazen imitations of his work. He felt flattered, rather than plagiarized, and gave me a lot of help."

"So he's a mentor. Like Roscoe Kane."

I lifted a lecturing finger. "There's a difference. . . . Kane's dead. Curt's alive."

"One of your few surviving heroes, then."

"Yup. So I'll cut him some slack any ole time."

Nearby, Tom Sardini was chatting with Mary Wright; both of them were in costume—Tom in his trenchcoat and fedora, Mary in a slinky shiny red low-cut gown that showed her figure off to good advantage.

"The Quakers wouldn't approve," I said, nodding toward her impressive decolletage.

"To hell with the Quakers," Mary said, toasting us with her plastic glass of ginger ale, slipping her arm around my shoulder mock-drunkenly and as if we were (ahem) bosom buddies.

Jill pinched me; the plaid suit was so heavy I barely felt it, though I got the point.

Jill said to her, coldly, "I didn't know you were an author."

"I'm not," Mary said, her arm still around my shoulder, as she paid Jill's manner no noticeable heed. "But a few of the roles had to be filled by Mohonk staff members."

I smiled and slipped out from Mary's arm as gracefully as possible and got Jill and myself some more ginger ale. We were standing sipping it when Cynthia Crystal slid over and put her arm around me; she seemed seductive despite her costume and makeup: she had transformed herself into a grandmother type, hair in a gray bun, wearing granny glasses and a blue calico Mother Hubbard.

"What big eyes you have, Granny," I said.

"Was I rude this morning?" she said.

"A little."

"Did it surprise you?"

"Not in the least."

She let loose her brittle laugh. "You really have me pegged, don't you, Mal?"

"I think so," I said with a lecherous grin. "But I love you anyway, Cynthia."

Jill pinched me again; this time she found her way under my coat to my pink shirt, under which was my pink flesh.

"Ow," I said.

"What?" Cynthia said.

"Nothing. Where's your Mr. Culver?"

She nodded over toward the fireplace. "Talking with his brother."

So he was. Culver was dressed all in black; what separated him from Johnny Cash were gloves, a beret, and a domino mask. Between the brothers, making a strange backdrop, was an oil painting in a fancy frame, leaned up above the fireplace, on the mantle—a striking abstract work in which shades of orange and yellow and red swirled in an off-center spiral, a whirlpool of color.

"What happened to their famous family feud?" I said.

"Fizzled, finally," Cynthia alliterated. She adjusted her granny wig. "It was mostly jealousy, you know."

Curt had had great success in Hollywood with his comedy caper novels, five of which had been made into movies and God only knew how many more of which had been optioned. But the critics had always been tough on Curt—unfairly, I thought—often referring to him as "a road company Donald E. Westlake." On the other hand, Tim Culver had earned kudos from even the toughest critics for his series about professional thief McClain; the acclaim included multiple Edgars and overseas awards. But in over a twenty-year career, he had never had any success in Hollywood—never generated a dime of option money (I knew the feeling).

"Tim envied Curt's financial success," Cynthia said, with a shrugging smile, "and Curt envied Tim's critical success."

"What turned that around?" Jill asked Cynthia. "They seem to be getting along now."

And they did. They were chatting, even smiling a little. Not warm; cool as the unlit fireplace, actually. But not feuding. One having invited the other, and the other having accepted.

"Tim sold McClain to the movies," Cynthia explained.

"Lawrence Kasdan took an option on the whole series, and the first of them, *McClain's Score*, is in preproduction now."

"Lawrence Kasdan," Jill said. "*Body Heat!* Wow!"

"Movie buff," I explained to Cynthia. "Ignore her. She won't take me seriously until *I* sell to the movies."

"You *did* sell to the movies," Cynthia said.

"TV doesn't count," Jill said.

"Especially at Mohonk," I added. "But as for the brotherly feud—am I right to assume that the glowing reviews Kirk Rath lavished on Curt helped smooth things over between him and Tim?"

"It certainly did," Cynthia confirmed. "Rath may not be liked—scratch the 'may'—but he *is* influential.

Other reviewers pay attention to him and the *Chronicler*; a lot of critics have been reassessing Curt's work since Kirk started championing him."

"So he and Tim," I said, "have no reason to be jealous of each other anymore."

"Happy ending, darling," Cynthia said, with her best cocktail party smile.

Jack Flint lumbered over, like a small tank; he was dressed as I'd seen him this morning—seemed not to be in costume. On closer look, he had extra gold chains around his neck; otherwise, business as usual.

He answered my unasked question with a shrug, saying, "The character I'm playing is so close to me, I didn't bother with dressing up. My wife, on the other hand, is *not* cast to type."

I looked around for her, and finally spotted Janis, sitting in a chair to one side; frankly, I felt she *had* been typecast: the outside of her had just been made to match her shy, quiet, inner nature; her cheery, bright California dresses had been replaced with a drab brown one. Her hair was pulled back and she wore no makeup.

I went over to her. "Nervous?"

Her smile was just a slight pulling back of the upper lip over tiny teeth. "Terrified."

"Don't be. The game is the thing, here. Our performances don't need to be Oscar level. Besides, aren't you a teacher? You should be used to being in front of people."

"I got out of teaching," she said. "It made me nervous, too."

"You're still in education, though."

"Yes. I'm assistant principal, primary level." She smiled again. "Peter Principle, I suppose. I wasn't much of a teacher so I got kicked upstairs."

"I'm sure you do a fine job. And I'm sure you'll do fine today, too."

"You're a nice man, Mr. Mallory."

"Call me Mal. And today I'm not a man, in case you haven't noticed."

"You seem to be more a mouse."

"I do at that."

She smiled more broadly now. "They really gave you a ribbing about that prank last night."

"They sure did."

"I wish it were true."

"What?"

"What you saw last night. That, or this mystery we're acting out."

"In what sense?"

She talked through her tiny teeth. "In the sense that that awful little bastard Kirk Rath would really be dead."

"Oh. That sense."

Still waters run deep.

I wished her luck with her performance and wandered back to Jill, who was talking with Cynthia and getting along well.

"I don't see Curt's wife anywhere," I said.

"She's in the loo," Cynthia said. Cynthia was the only person I knew who would use that expression. "Putting the finishing touches on her makeup and costume. Oh. There she is, now. . . ."

And there she was.

Poured into a slinky black gown. Like Mary Wright, her figure was shown off to great advantage. Kim was slightly top-heavy, and a lot of creamy skin was showing.

"I'm just looking," I said to Jill. "No pinching, please."

"We'll just both keep our hands to ourselves," Jill said agreeably.

Kim's eyes locked on mine and she grinned and, snugging her tight dress in place on the way, she came over to us. I hadn't seen her since my last New York trip the year before.

"I *hate* tight clothes," she said, not at all coy, as if she were unaware the clinging dress made the most of her voluptuous figure. She had a high, slightly breathy, Judy Holliday sort of voice, and exaggerated Madeline Kahn features, which landed her a lot of second female leads in Neil Simon comedies on the bus-and-truck circuit. Kim had only been in one Broadway production, and then late in its run, though she'd appeared in several off-Broadway shows.

I introduced Jill to her, and Jill immediately started asking her what films she'd been in. Kim had some impressive credits—everything from *King of Comedy* to *The Muppets Take Manhattan*—but she'd only done extra work in them. Jill was wowed anyway. Then Pete Christian, dressed to the nines in a rented tux, stole Jill away to talk film buff talk.

Kim smiled like an ornery kid and said, "I hear somebody auditioned for you last night."

"Out my window, you mean."

She nodded, batted her big brown eyes. "I've heard of off off-Broadway, but this is ridiculous."

"Ridiculous is right."

"You make a *fabulous* nerd, Mal."

"Gee, thanks. Have you been working, Kim?"

"Here and there. I'm curtailing the roadshows for a while."

"Why's that?"

She smiled a little, not showing her teeth. "Curt and I are buying a little house in Connecticut. After five years of marriage, we're finally going the whole domestic route."

"I thought you'd stay in Greenwich Village forever. Surely you're not giving up the stage?"

"No! Just the traveling. And the Village is getting a little lavender for Curt's taste. Anyway, I can commute to Manhattan for any theatrical or TV work that comes along."

"Does 'going the whole domestic route' mean to imply that you and Curt are expecting an addition to the family. . . ?"

"Not yet," she said. Smiling a little. Then, in a whisper: "But we are trying."

"Well, that's great, Kim."

She got serious all of a sudden. "It would mean a lot to Curt. He . . . he lost Gary six months ago, you know."

Gary was his son, his only child, by his first marriage; his wife Joan had died in an automobile crash seven years ago. The novel he wrote thereafter—*It Feels So Good When You Stop*—was his first brush with critical acceptance; it had dealt, in a tragicomic manner, with the loss of Joan.

As for Gary, I'd never met him; knew nothing about him, except that he was an artist and Curt was proud of him.

"When you say 'lost'. . ."

"I mean dead," she said, with a sad shrug. "Pneumonia."

"Damn. Aw, shit."

"Curt took it pretty hard; but he's getting over it. He's working on a book, after a dry spell of a few months, and he took on this Mohonk weekend, at Mary Wright's urging."

"I wish I'd known," I said. "I feel awful, not giving him any support. . . ."

"You know Curt. He's very open in some senses, but private in others."

"Aw, damn. I'm so removed, living in Iowa. Something like this happens to a friend and I don't even hear about it till six months later."

She touched my arm. "Don't give it another thought."

"Is it too late for me to express my sympathy?"

"No. Not if you find the right time. It's still very much on Curt's mind. You saw the painting over the fireplace?"

"Yes, I did. Is that one of Gary's?"

She looked over at it, smiling in a bittersweet way, nodding. "Curt won't go anywhere without one of Gary's paintings along."

"That's really sad."

"I don't think so," she said cheerily. "He doesn't stare broodingly at it," she went on, nodding toward the swirling, fiery painting above the unlit fireplace, "but it comforts him having a part of his son in the room with him."

"I wish I'd known Gary."

"You'd have liked him, Mal. He was a lot of fun. Only twenty-six when he died ... and if that isn't a goddamn shame I don't know what is."

"Nor do I."

Curt came over and said, "I see you're putting the make on my young bride."

I gave him a lopsided smile. "How else can I get back at you for spreading tales about me?"

"Think twice about dallying, my dear," he said to Kim. "Would you really want our first born to look like, that?" And he pointed to my nerdy countenance.

I had no snappy comeback for that, and, even if I had, it would have done no good: Curt was now moving toward the center of the room, and began waving his hands, impressario-like.

"Showtime!" he shouted, and the room quieted down. "If you don't know where you're supposed to be positioned for your interrogation session, stop and ask me on the way out. Any other questions? No? Do you want to save the malt shop? Then let's put on a show! And like we say in show business—not to mention the mystery biz—*knock 'em dead!*"

9
. . .

I ignored the plush, plump loveseats and the velvet cushioned armchairs and went directly for a straight-back chair in one corner of the little open parlor, one of several on the second floor, off a wide, open hall. Morning light filtered in through the sheer-curtained windows, bounced lazily off the mirror over the fireplace. Glasses perched midway down my nose, bow tie straight, hair slick, I sat with my legs together, hunched a bit, striving to be inconspicuous. But the SUSPECT badge on my plaid suit gave me away.

"Are you Lester?" asked a young woman with short hair, glasses, and a red sweater. A short, plump woman in a blue sweater was with her.

"Yes," I said timidly.

"Lester," the young woman said, smiling warmly but with eagerness in her eyes, "could I ask you a few questions?"

"Yes," I said woefully.

And the interrogators began to file in, some taking chairs, others standing, others plopping down on couches, but none of them leaning back—all angled forward, backs straight as boards, notebooks at the ready, expressions as alert as hunting dogs. Like reporters in a press conference, they began hurling questions at me, sometimes stepping on each other's toes, verbally. They were members of competing teams, after all.

"When did you last see Roark K. Sloth alive?" an intense man in glasses and gray sweater asked.

"Last night," I said.

"What were the circumstances?"

I swallowed. "Unpleasant."

Some of them laughed at that; others seemed impatient with me. Time was precious, after all. But I made them dig for each truffle and, piece by piece, they were able to draw forth from me the story in Curt's script. I held back only on the bribe, which I figured to reveal in the second of the sessions, tomorrow morning.

"Did you see anyone else entering or leaving Sloth's room?" a guy who looked almost as nerdy as me asked.

"No," I said. "But . . . well, it's not really my place to gossip."

A woman in a red and white sweater was amused by that, but followed up. "No, Lester. Go on. We're interested in anything you saw that might be helpful."

"Well . . ." I leaned forward conspiratorially. "I did see that private detective—that Darsini person—walking in the hall as I departed. He might have been going to Mr. Sloth's room."

"Were you aware that Darsini was in Sloth's employ?"

"No," I said.

"When did you find out about Sloth's death?"

"This morning. The police came to my room to question me."

The intense guy in gray pointed a pencil at me and made an accusation. "Isn't it true that you saw Sloth murdered outside your window last night?"

That threw me. I'd done a pretty good job, I thought, of settling into the nerdy persona of Lester Denton; I'd even done a pretty fair job of putting Kirk Rath, and what may or may not have happened to him, outside my mind for a time.

But the story of the so-called prank last night had obviously found its way beyond the inner circle of authors and out into the mainstream of Mystery Weekenders, who (at least some of them) were dealing with what I'd seen as if it were a part of Curt's staged mystery. And I didn't quite know how to handle that.

Meanwhile, the intense guy in gray was doing his Hamilton Burger impression. "Answer the question, Mr. Denton!"

"I did," I said. Or Lester said. "I did see it. But I must have been dreaming. I reported what I saw to the hotel staff, but when we went outside, there was no corpse in the snow. I must have imagined it."

"Did you tell the police about this?" another interrogator asked.

Now I was floundering. I had done pretty well, as long as I had Curt's script to lean on; but now that I had allowed myself to wander from it, I was no longer swimming; I was treading water, and not terribly well.

"The hotel manager told them about it," I said. "And they questioned me, yes. But, as I told them, if I were involved somehow, why would I go to the front desk to report what I'd seen?"

The guy in gray was pointing his pencil at me again. "Yet you saw him killed with a *knife*—and that is precisely the way he *was* killed."

He was just obnoxious enough to make me glad he was wasting his time down this blind alley.

"Excuse me for my boldness," I said, "but wasn't Mr. Sloth's body found in his room, sitting at his . . . its . . . typewriter?"

"Yes," said the guy in gray. "But the coroner has established time of death as late last night—corresponding with what you saw!"

I didn't know what to say. I'd been trying to explain away the prank (or whatever it was) within the context of the fictional mystery they sought to solve, because otherwise it would only serve to throw them unfairly off their game. But we weren't supposed to break character during the Interrogation Sessions, so stopping to explain (as Mallory) seemed out of the question.

And speaking of questions . . .

An attractive brunette in black said, "Are you Jewish, Mr. Denton?"

Was I? Curt hadn't said. I winged it: "No, ma'am. But some of my best friends are."

I—or Lester—got a little laugh out of that one.

"But do you speak or read Yiddish, Mr. Denton?" she continued. "Or are conversant with any dialect related to Yiddish?"

"No, ma'am."

"So you couldn't translate the phrase, 'tovl fof oy'?"

"No, ma'am."

And we seemed to be off the subject of what I—or Lester or anybody—had seen out my (his/her/their) window last night.

As the questioning continued, various interrogators left, while fresh blood filled in. Each team had assigned one or two members to be at each of the suspect's grillings, and when their team representatives deemed a suspect sufficiently grilled, they were free to move on and help grill another one.

But my grilling was over; the hour was up.

I smiled and took off my bow tie and said, "Lester isn't here anymore."

There were some expressions of frustration, but mostly laughs and even a little applause. People were smiling; they'd all had a good time, except for the anal retentives like the guy in gray, who were taking this charade a bit too seriously. This was supposed to be a vacation, after all. What the hell was relaxing about trading the pressure of your work for the pressure of some goddamn game?

The attractive brunette who'd asked the question about Yiddish stopped to shake my hand. She had sharp but pretty features, and jade-green eyes.

"You were terrific," she said. "You make Ed Grimley look like a macho man."

Her reference was to a Second City character created by Martin Short, which led me to compliment her on her taste.

"I'm a big Second City fan myself," I said.

"TV or stage?"

"Both. I've seen various Chicago companies, oh, I bet a dozen times; and a couple of the Toronto companies, including the one that seeded the original 'Saturday Night Live.' "

"Are you an actor yourself?"

"No, no. I'm strictly a writer."

She seemed a little embarrassed. "Well, I know you're a writer; it's just that your performance as Lester made me wonder if you'd had professional training."

"The last play I was in was *My Fair Lady* in high school."

She laughed a little. "You know, I have to admit I've never read anything of yours, but I plan to remedy that."

"That's nice to hear. And, I must say, you're a very attractive young woman. I make that observation well realizing that the sturdy young man lurking behind you is very likely your boyfriend."

"Husband," she said, smiling; she motioned for him to step forward, and he did. Like her, he was in his late twenties; blond, handsome in a preppy way, sweater and Calvins; they were as perfect as a couple in a toothpaste ad.

"I'm Jenny Logan," she said, offering a hand to shake, which I took. "And this is my husband, Frank."

I shook Frank's hand too; he had a firm grip and a white, if shy, smile.

"*You* wouldn't happen to be in show biz, would you?" I asked them.

"Frank's a lawyer," she said, patting his shoulder fondly. "But he doesn't do trial work, so I guess you'd have to say he's not in show biz. I, however, am."

"In New York?"

"Yes. Mostly commercials."

Maybe I *had* seen her in a toothpaste ad.

"Could I talk to you two, for a moment?" I said, even though I already was. I gestured toward a comfortable-looking velvet couch near a baby grand piano.

We sat, Jenny in the middle.

"Have you ever been to Mystery Weekend at Mohonk before?" I asked them.

Frank nodded, but Jenny lit up, all smiles and enthusiasm.

"Oh yes, and it's great!" Jenny said, like the captain of the Mohonk cheerleaders. Then she forced herself to calm down: "At least *I* think it's great. Frank isn't a puzzle freak like I am—though he figured last year's out, darn him."

"Your team was one of the winners?"

"Yes," she said. "Funny thing is, we were going all out to win 'most creative,' and thanks to Frank, here, we won for accuracy!"

"Attaboy, Frank," I said. "What are you going after *this* year?"

"Whatever we can get, Mr. Mallory," Frank said, smiling, proving he could speak.

"Make it Mal," I said. "And I was just wondering if you'd brought any theatrical gear along."

She shrugged. "A little. Some makeup and such. It'd be nice to bring more—all sorts of props and stuff. It'd really help score points in the 'most creative' category. But it's hard to know what to bring, since we don't know what the mystery's going to be till we get here."

"I want to ask you something," I said. "And I promise if you'll be truthful, you won't get into any trouble."

Jenny narrowed her eyes, leaned her head forward. "Trouble?"

"I would greatly appreciate it if you'd put my mind to rest and admit to what you did last night."

Frank grinned. "Is that really necessary? We *are* married, you know."

"I'm not kidding around," I said. "Was it you?"

Jenny was shaking her head. "I really don't know what you're talking about, Mal."

"You heard me being questioned about 'Sloth' being killed outside my window, last night."

"Yes . . ."

"Well, something did happen outside my window last night."

"We know," Jenny said, shrugging again.

"You know?"

"Everybody's talking about it," she said. "It's part of the weekend, right? Something Curt Clark staged to get things off with a bang?"

I sighed. "If Curt staged it," I said, "he's keeping me in the dark. He says it's a prank pulled by one of the teams."

"Oh!" Jenny said. "I get it. You thought *we* might

have been the ones behind it ... but we weren't. I swear."

"Don't kid around with me, please."

Frank said. "We're not. Are you sure this isn't Clark's doing? Part of his weekend?"

"I was very upset last night," I said, "and we're good friends, Curt and I. He has a nasty sense of humor, granted. But he would've told me."

Ever suspicious, like any true Mystery Weekender, Jenny said, "Where was he when the prank was pulled?"

"He was in his room," I said. "I'd spoken to him on the phone, moments before. He just didn't have time to get outside, even if he climbed out a window. Besides, the 'killer' was a short, stocky person; and of course Curt's lanky and tall."

"You're telling us," she said, surprised, "that this isn't part of the mystery."

"That's right," I said. "When somebody brought it up during the interrogation, I tried to deflect it, but I only helped things to get more out of hand."

"So we know something the other teams don't," she said, with a smug, squeezed smile.

"Yes," I said. "Though I wouldn't mind it spreading to the other teams."

"No way," she said, with a wave of finality. "Let 'em do their own investigating."

Brother.

"I'd like to ask a favor of you," I said.

She shrugged. "Sure. As long as it doesn't help out some other team."

"Well, it does involve the other teams: do you know if any of them have theatrical pros on them?"

"A few that I know of do," Jenny nodded. "I could ask around a bit. See if anybody wants to pool props and makeup. You'd like to know if any of the other teams staged that 'murder,' I take it?"

"That's right," I said.

"What's in it for us?" she said, with an evil little smile. "Will you tell us whether or not you're the killer?"

"No," I said. "But I will do this for you: I won't tell any other game-players that the prank isn't a part of Curt's mystery. That'll give your team one up on everybody else."

"Deal," she said, and we shook hands.

They got up and wandered off, Jenny glancing back and reminding me that if I didn't keep my end of the bargain, I'd have to talk to her lawyer; and Jill sat down.

"Who was the dish you were talking to?" she said.

"Don't pinch me again, please, I think I'd cry."

"I meant the guy," she said.

I smiled and shook my head and filled her in. "How were the other interrogation sessions?"

"Interesting," she said, her tan face impassive. "I don't have any insights into your fellow suspects, though, I'm afraid. Nobody seemed particularly nervous, including Janis Flint. But one funny thing . . . did you know that what happened outside our window last night is getting itself worked into the weekend mystery?"

"Tell me about it," I sighed. "I tried to do some fancy footwork around that and fell all over my feet. How'd the other suspects do, fielding it?"

She lifted one eyebrow for a moment. "A couple of them, it really threw. Specifically, Tom and Pete. Tom actually broke character for a moment and said he didn't know anything about that."

"Hmmm. How about the questioners?"

"I've got the names of a few intense types written down in my little notebook."

"Good. Let's go back to the room; I want to try to call Rath again."

"Okay. Then some lunch, and then you have to give a little talk, right?"

"Right."

"And then maybe we can bust out of this joint."

"I don't think so. I'm supposed to be on a panel after that, filling in for the missing Mr. Rath."

"No you aren't," she said, with a certain glee. "Tom told me to tell you his private-eye panel won't be till tomorrow afternoon; Curt's own talk has been moved up in its place. So it's official. We're going over the wall, pal."

I sat up; sought to be a man despite my nebbish exterior. "Oh yeah? You're not going to drag me along on some damn *nature* hike, are you?"

"I most certainly am."

"Jill, you disappoint me. What was the first thing the pioneers did when they got to the wilderness?"

"I know, I know. They built a cabin and went inside. You've told me a million times. But I'm not standing for being cooped up all afternoon with these mystery maniacs and puzzle paranoids—not when there's a big beautiful outdoors waiting for us out there!"

"Okay. But you owe me one."

She looped her arm in mine and batted her cornflower blues. "Sure. You can collect right now, back in the room."

"Before lunch?"

"Why not? But you have to promise me one thing."

"And what's that?"

"You'll leave the little mustache *on*. . . ."

10

• • •

The Mohonk Hiker's Map listed Sky Top as a "moderate walk" (as opposed to those walks labelled "short and easy" or "strenuous"). If this was a moderate walk, Mussolini was a benevolent dictator.

Of course, just on general principles, I hate the Great Out-of-Doors. I grew up on a farm, and from my early childhood swore I would one day live in the city—Port City, as it turned out, but that counts, technically at least. Will Rogers said he never met a man he didn't like; I never milked a cow I liked.

The last period of my life during which I spent an inordinate amount of time in the Great Out-of-Doors was a place called Vietnam, where roughing it meant something other than a Winnebago and a six-pack of Bud. Camping trips don't appeal much to those of us whose boondockers got soggy in a rice paddy. I swore to myself if I ever got back on good old dry American soil I'd spend as much time as possible indoors. Or, as I like to put it, the Great Indoors.

If this seems irrational and rambling, well, so was my state of mind as I climbed with the lovely Jill Forrest—whose very name suggests a kinship to trees, and she can have them—making our way up a seemingly ever-narrowing path with the mountaintop our goal.

Why does one climb such a path? To get to the top. And what does one do once one gets there? One hikes back to the bottom. Ask me why I do not want to climb a mountain and I will tell you simply: because it's there.

"Quit grumbling," she said, a few steps ahead of me but not, unfortunately for her, out of earshot. Her rear end looked cute in the black ski pants, which matched her black ski jacket, which matched her black-and-white stocking cap.

"I hate this," I said. My jacket wasn't wintry enough and, even with the sweater on underneath it, I was cold. The path, which had begun deceptively wide, now left barely room for two people; my legs ached from walking on this bed of snow-dusted pine needles and twigs and rocks.

"No kidding."

"Let's turn back. The snow's really coming down."

And it was. Not a blizzard, but it had been lightly snowing all day, and it did seem to be picking up.

"Sissy," she said.

"No, really," I said. "There's some ice in it. If it keeps at it, we could have a rough time getting back down, once we get up. By rough I mean slippery."

And, I should point out, that while at our left was a forest not unlike Jill's last name, at our right were a few rocks and a whole lot of drop-off. Of the plummeting-to-the-earth-flailing-your-arms-and-legs-and-screaming-holy-hell-all-the-way-down variety.

"Don't be silly," she said, stepping on one of the roots

that served as a step and slipping just a little, despite her boots. I caught her, even though I was wearing Hush Puppies, and she looked back at me and, with friendly malice, stuck out her tongue. She got snow on it.

"Let's go back," I said.

"No! We'll rest a minute."

Well, I needed the rest—we were probably halfway up this goddamn glandular-case hill, and I had shin splints and sore calves—but, as I pointed out to her, pausing to rest would only allow the snow to gain on us.

"Coward," she said, and veered off from the path to the right—you remember the right: a sheer drop-off to nothingness?—across some boulders to a gazebo, where she plopped her pretty butt down on the rough wooden bench and waited for me to develop the *cojones* to join her.

I did, finally, even if my *cojones* hadn't yet developed, and if they hadn't by my age they were unlikely to, and we sat and squinted down at a cold, gray, but eerily beautiful vista that included the blue-gray expanse of frozen Mohonk Lake and the oversize Victorian dollhouse that was the hotel. Mountain house.

"Takes your breath away," she said.

"So does a seven-hundred-foot fall."

She pursed her lips in a smirk. "You're so romantic."

"I'm so cold. Let's press on."

We both slipped a little on the boulders, heading back for the path, where I pointed out the snow was undisturbed.

"So?" she asked, taking the lead again.

"So, we're the only ones today foolhardy enough to make this trek, in the snow, in the cold."

She glanced back. "That's because the hotel is filled with crazy people. They don't want to enjoy the scenery. They don't want to drink in God's grandeur."

"You can't drink it if it's frozen.'

"They," she continued, ignoring me, not glancing back anymore, "would rather stay inside and try to solve some phony mystery."

I didn't quite understand the appeal of that, either, but I didn't admit it to Jill; I had enjoyed playing a suspect, but playing detective—if the crime wasn't real, anyway—held no fascination for me.

"They," she continued to continue, "would rather sit in a drafty hall and listen to some pompous windbag talk about his theories on mystery writing."

"Low blow!" I said.

"You wish," she said. And now she glanced back, and her smile would've been impish, if I were the kind of writer to use a word like "impish."

I caught up to her; there was just room enough on the snowy path to walk two abreast. Depending on the size of the breasts.

"I thought my little talk went pretty well," I said, in a mild pout.

She smiled warmly, despite the cold. "So did I, really. You were cute as lace pants."

"That's a Raymond Chandler line."

"I know. You had me reading *Farewell, My Lovely* last week, remember?"

"I remember. Did I really seem pompous?"

"Not at all. You were funny."

I *had* gotten a few good one-liners off. Not during the speech itself, which was a fairly serious discussion of the difficulties I'd encountered turning real crimes into fictional ones. In my case, some of my books were derived from my own life—crimes I'd been caught up in; times when I had played detective for real.

But the question-and-answer session had gone especially well, and that's where I managed to get a few laughs.

"Are you going to turn this weekend into a novel?" one of them had asked.

"Not unless I find a body," I'd said.

Which got a particularly nice laugh.

Only a part of me didn't find that so funny—the part that was still trying to figure out whether what I'd seen out my window last night was histrionics or homicide.

And, before my little speech in the big Parlor, where high windows looked out on the lake and pictures of old Smileys (the Mohonk founding family) looked down on me and my audience like the bearded faces on cough-drop packages, I had discovered something disturbing: Kirk Rath had indeed not made it home yet.

From our room I had called the business number at Rath's house and got one of his co-editors.

"No sign of Kirk here," he had said, followed by a nervous laugh. Whenever somebody from the *Chronicler* called me on the phone—which they did from time to time, to acquire publishing information for their news column—they invariably followed whatever they stated or asked with a nervous laugh. I read that as embarrass-ment out of having to deal face to face, even if it were over the phone, with another human being whose work they had inhumanly lambasted in their smug pages (and if you don't think a page can be smug, you've never read the *Chronicler*—even the ink is smug).

"Do you expect Kirk?" I asked him.

"No. He's on vacation this week."

"Well, he was here at Mohonk."

"Oh, you're calling from the resort?"

"Yes. And Kirk left here last night. I wondered if he'd gotten home yet."

"No, but then we don't expect him. He was going to go into New York City after Mohonk."

"Business?"

"No. Vacation. We don't even have a number to reach him."

"Does he do that often?"

"Now and then, Mallory. But why the questions?"

"I need to talk to him. Personal matter."

"Oh. Well, he may have told Rick Fahy where he was going."

"Rick Fahy . . . isn't he one of your contributers?"

"Yes. He's there at Mohonk, playing the mystery. We're going to do a story on the weekend from the point of view of an attendee."

"I've never met Fahy; I'll look him up and ask him."

"Fine. If Kirk does show up, would you like me to have him call you?"

"Yes, immediately. Here at Mohonk. My room number is sixty-four. I'll be here till Sunday afternoon."

I'd made one other call, to the guard who'd been on duty at the Gate House last night. Mary Wright had provided his number. He hadn't seen Rath leave, but that didn't necessarily mean Rath hadn't left.

"I log in every car that enters," he said, a young voice, college kid maybe, "but don't pay much attention to who leaves."

It seemed a good number of Mohonk employees were residents of nearby New Paltz, so a rather steady stream of them left during the evening hours. Rath, if he had left, left unnoticed.

Which meant my question about the reality, or lack thereof, of what I'd witnessed out my window remained no closer to being established. All this really nailed down was that Rath did not leave and come back through the Gate House, because if he had, he'd have been logged in.

And now I was in the Great Out-of-Doors, on a rocky, root-veined hard dirt path upon which icy snow was settling, only it was too late to turn back. We were almost there.

And in five minutes, we were. Our path merged with a crushed-rock road, a one-lane affair used by horses and service vehicles (our map called it a carriage road), which had wound its own way to Sky Top, that plateau where on a clear day you could see forever, or anyway New Jersey and four or five other states. This wasn't a clear day but, from the outcroppings of boulders along the edge, you could see a panorama of winter gray, broken up by evergreens, that did take the breath away, or maybe it was just the climb.

"Oh, Mal," Jill said, her gloved hand grasping mine. "Isn't it breathtaking!"

"Maybe it's just the climb," I offered, but I smiled at her.

Sky Top was a clearing about half the size of a football field, and in its midst was a tower of rough-cut stone, a fairly squat two-stories or so, with a spire that aspired to another story, capped by a gray-green helmet wearing a flag pole. No flag flew today, and when we tried the tower door, it was locked.

The crushed-rock carriage road extended around the tower, and as we strolled, gloved hand-in-hand, around it to try out another view from Sky Top, we noticed something.

A car.

A car parked on the carriage road, behind the tower. It was fairly well covered with snow, a sporty little dark blue Fiat. I tried the doors, but they were locked. I rubbed the frost from a side window and peered in. On the back seat a stack of magazines sat like a forgotten passenger.

The latest issue of *The Mystery Chronicler*, forty or fifty copies, probably.

"I think I know whose car this is," I said.

"What do you mean?" Jill asked; her eyes were wide.

"Let's have a look around."

We found him in one of the outcroppings of rocks. Like his car, he was fairly well covered with snow. The front of his jacket was slashed and blood was dried there, or frozen, or something. Dark and crusty, whatever it was. His face was slashed several times, and the wounds were not recent; they had snow in them, and were jagged and crusted with black blood, but the features were recognizable.

It was Kirk S. Rath, all right.

And Jill, not being a stereotypical female, did not scream; neither did I. I'd seen dead bodies before. I'd even seen this dead body before. I bent over him, poked at him a bit: no question he was gone. There seemed to be two deep wounds in his chest; those stab wounds, not the facial slashes, had killed him. Rath's face seemed oddly passive, for having been slashed; peaceful, youthful, though older than this you don't get. I checked his pockets. His billfold, containing several hundred dollars in cash, was intact in his back pocket. The envelope in which he'd received his mystery weekend instructions was folded in his pocket; in it was the list of the suspects in his—or Roark K. Sloth's—murder.

Then I backed away from him. Away from the rocks, away from the drop-off, away from the long, cold fall. For all my bitching, I hadn't noticed the sound of the storm till now; but now the wind seemed to be fairly screaming. The snow was really coming down, now, and there was indeed ice in it. Crystals glistened on the slashed face of the corpse sprawled on Sky Top's rocks.

Jill and I stood shivering together, not entirely from the cold, and then started down. The map suggested walking the carriage path on the return, for a "gentler" return trip. But our near-panic and the increasing snow and the steepness of the way had us stumbling, sliding. By the time the carriage road intersected with Sky Top Path at the foot of the mountain, we were walking through a blizzard. We were just about to really panic when suddenly the Mountain House loomed before us.

11

• • •

We stood under the bare beams of the east porch, breathing hard and smoky, shaking the snow off our clothes onto the bare gray wooden slats beneath us. Despite the blizzard out there, the direction of the wind was such that the floor of the open porch was barely dusted with white, when I'd expected it to be drifted. Which it soon would be—the wind was whirling and would get around to it; the lake already was gone, its gray-blue surface buried beneath the white. Faces in the windows along the porch stared out into the ever-whitening world, some awestruck, others indifferent, while below the windows countless rocking chairs made a wooden chorus line. This time of year no one sat out in them, not in this cold, so the chairs were turned on end, rockers up, like a row of curved yellowed tusks in some elephant's graveyard.

We stamped the snow from our feet on the mats inside the porch doors, but didn't take off our outer winter clothing, barreling right on into the Lake Lounge, where Curt Clark was giving an informal question-and-answer session during the traditional Mohonk afternoon "tea"—cookies and cups, very genteel. Just like in a British drawing-room mystery.

Only I didn't remember grotesquely maimed corpses like Kirk Rath's showing up in such polite mysteries; or, if they did, the author would present an image considerably more tasteful than the police-photo accurate dead-body picture that was burned in my brain like a concentration camp tattoo.

Curt glanced at me, smiled, squinted, not knowing what to make of our barging in, all bundled up and with winter dandruff on our shoulders. A hundred or so Mystery Weekenders were seated at tables and some again sat Indian-style on the floor as he stood before them fielding their questions, one of which he was currently in the process of answering: "So, while you may find it hard to accept, there are several movie versions of my novels that I have not seen. That I refuse to see. Friends have warned me off them. And I trust my friends."

Upon the word "friends" he had glanced at me, squinting again, shaking his head in some unasked question. Perhaps my expression was sufficiently grave to tell him something was up; I glanced at Jill and her expression told nothing—like the Great-Out-of-Doors we'd just left behind us, her face was frozen.

Mary Wright, in a blue Mohonk blazer (its symbol—a tiny gazebo—on one breast pocket) and a white blouse with a blue ascot, approached us, looking confused and a little put out. Curt was, in the meantime, fielding another question. Mary smiled, but it was a strain; you just don't walk into the Lake Lounge all wet and snowy.

"Is something wrong?" Mary asked, giving us the benefit of the doubt.

"Yes," I said. "Perhaps we should talk in your office."

"All right. Should Curt be there? If I read your tone of voice correctly, this is something serious."

"Yes."

She took me by the arm, huddled close. "Does it affect our weekend?"

"Oh yes."

"Let me get Curt, then. He's almost finished with this . . ."

Jill looked at her with flat dislike and said, "This can't wait, honey."

Mary let go of my arm and smiled at Jill. It was a smile that had nothing to do with humor or goodwill or cheerfulness. It was a smile that had a lot to do with one woman not appreciating another woman calling her "honey."

"Mohonk moves at its own pace, dear," she said to Jill. "No crisis is going to ruffle *our* composure. Understood?"

Jill just looked at her. She didn't like being called "dear" anymore than Mary liked being called "honey."

Curt was saying, "And I think that about wraps it up. The rest of the afternoon is open for you to begin sorting through the information you gathered at this morning's interrogations. Just remember the Mystery Writers of America's slogan—'Crime doesn't pay . . . enough.' "

A ripple of laughter was followed by applause, and Curt moved rather more quickly through the crowd than he might otherwise have, not pausing to chat or sign any of the books of his which various guests had brought along to the session. He knew something was afoot.

"What is it, Mal?"

"Not here," I said. "Ms. Wright's office?"

"It's Miss," she said, and smiled at me.

"There's been a fucking murder," Jill almost hissed. Nobody heard it but Mary and Curt and me, but she'd made her point.

Mary wasn't shocked by Jill's profanity, Mohonk manners, Quaker tradition, or not. But she did purse her lips in a skeptical smile and narrow her eyes the same way ... but only for a moment. Our expressions apparently were ominous enough to get the point across.

Not to Curt, though.

"Mal," he said, grinning, "if you're pulling some cute counter-prank and making us the butt—"

"Let's go to Miss Wright's office," I said. "Now."

Curt pushed the air with his palms in a conciliatory manner. "Settle down, settle down. We'll go to my suite. It's closer, and we can have a drink. Mary's office is shockingly short on Scotch."

We walked wordlessly down the corridor, Jill unzipping her ski jacket, climbing out of it, her face blank, but blank in a way that I knew meant anger. Whether the cause of that was the intrusion of Rath's death upon our more or less pleasant afternoon, or her dislike of Mary Wright, I couldn't say. And I wasn't about to ask.

Curt unlocked the room. We stood out in the hall as he went in. I caught a glimpse of his wife Kim, napping on the bed in a lacy slip, her bosom half-spilling out, heaving with sleep; she was a beautiful woman, but I didn't give a damn. Violent death puts a damper on my libido.

A few minutes later, Kim exited, wearing a turtleneck sweater and slacks and a dazed expression. She smiled sleepily.

"Curt said you wanted some privacy," she said. "Ours is not to reason why. . . ." And she shrugged and waved and went away.

We went in. I unsnapped my jacket and found a chair

to lay it on. Curt was pouring himself a glass of Scotch over at the table that served as a makeshift bar. Some vodka and bourbon and various bottles of soda were there as well.

"Can I get anyone anything?" he asked.

Mary Wright said no, and Jill went over and poured herself a couple fingers of bourbon. I asked him for some Scotch.

"On the rocks?" he asked.

Boy did *that* conjure the wrong image. I shivered and said, "Straight up will do. Just a little. I just want to warm up inside."

Jill stood looking at the orange and yellow and red painting that leaned in its frame against the wall above the fireplace; its whirlpool effect seemed to draw her in. Then she pulled away and downed the bourbon in a couple of belts.

Curt sat on the edge of the bed, swirling his Scotch in his glass; Mary Wright stood nearby. So did I. Jill and her Bourbon lurked back by the painting.

"Mal," Curt said. "Before we get into this, I'd like to say I can understand your wanting to stage some sort of reprisal. You're stubborn and you don't like to be had. I can understand that. But you're having fun this weekend, aren't you? Let it go at that."

Mary said, "What are you talking about?"

Curt said, "Do you mind if I tell her?"

"Go ahead," I said.

And he did. His version, of course, treated what I'd seen last night out my window as if its being a prank were an established fact.

But when he finished, I said, "What I saw was not a prank. Kirk Rath really is dead."

Curt smirked and sighed as if both amused and frustrated by the behavior of an irrepressible child; Mary

Wright's eyes again narrowed, and she tilted her head to one side, brunette hair swinging.

I told them, slowly, carefully, what Jill and I had seen.

"You're serious," Curt said, though not sure yet.

"Deadly fucking," I said.

"Quit saying that word," Mary said, suddenly irritated.

"*I'm* the one who said it before," Jill said.

Mary whirled on Jill. "Why don't you just shut up?"

Jill said, "What are you going to do about it?"

"What do you *want* me to do? Pull your *hair* out?"

"I mean about the murder," Jill said. Hands on her hips. "Don't lose your composure, dear."

Mary had nothing to say to that. Her face fell, and her rage went with it. Ashen, she sat on the bed next to Curt; they looked like lovers in the midst of a bedroom quarrel, not sure what move to make next. Curt had one hand on one of his knees, the other, with the Scotch, was in his lap. He was studying me.

"You *are* serious," he said, as if he didn't believe his own words. "This is not a joke."

"It's not a joke. It's not a goddamn joke! Do we look like we're kidding? Are either of us that good an actor?"

He looked at me hard and then he stood; Mary continued to sit, lost in worry.

He came and put a hand on my shoulder. "I'm sorry. I shouldn't have laughed off what you told me before." He was shaking his head; he seemed embarrassed and bewildered. "What can I say? I steered you wrong."

"I can see how you thought what you thought," I said. "I've been around these people today. I've seen how caught up in their game they are. How obsessive they are about it. I can see why you figured it for a prank."

"But it wasn't a prank," Jill said. She was over pouring herself some more bourbon.

"So it would seem," Curt said, shaking his head, more in amazement than bewilderment now.

"I should call the police," Mary said, sick about it.

"Yes you should," I said.

She used Curt's phone. Before long she was talking to somebody called Chief Colby. I wondered if that meant he was head cheese.

Soon I was talking to the chief, filling him in.

"You're a good observer, Mr. Mallory," he said.

"Thank you. What do we do now?"

"Wait there at the mountain house. We'll be right up."

I hung up the phone. Outside the wind was rattling the windows, whistling through its teeth.

"Cops are on the way," I said.

"Good," Jill said.

"They'll have a hell of a time," I said, "getting up to Sky Top now."

"It really is coming down," Curt said with a fatalistic shrug, looking out the frosted window at the snow. "What was he doing back here?"

"Who?"

"Who do you think? Rath. He left last night—why did he come back and get himself killed?"

"I don't know," I admitted. "Maybe he only pretended to leave."

"But why?" Curt asked. "And why would somebody kill him Thursday night, outside your window, in the broad moonlight, and then lug him up to Sky Top?"

"Beats me," I said. "Hell of a place to hide a corpse—right out in the open where the next hiker will find him."

"Whoever did it," Jill said, "hauled the corpse up in

Rath's own car. Maybe to get both of them out of sight, just for the moment."

"Just for that evening," Curt said, nodding. "Perhaps the murderer did his—or her—deed and then took off."

Mary seemed to perk up, just a bit. "You mean it wasn't necessarily someone who was here for the Mystery Weekend?"

"Not necessarily," I agreed. "It could have been somebody who followed him here, or came looking for him. His co-workers knew where he was going; it was no secret."

The phone rang. Curt answered it, then held it out for Mary. "It's for you."

"Yes?" she said. "Yes? Oh . . . oh, really. Well, I'm not surprised. . . . Yes, well, thank you." She hung up and sighed and looked around the room at all of us, including Jill, shrugged elaborately and said, "That was the Gate House. The road up the mountain's been shut down."

Nobody said anything.

"It's not passable," she said, shrugging again. "It's heavily drifted, over a sheet of ice. And it's still coming down."

I held out my open palms to her. "Don't you have plows . . .?"

"Yes," she said. "And they're not getting anywhere. It'll be hours—maybe longer—before we can get that road cleared. Until it stops snowing, we won't even try."

"What!"

"Mr. Mallory," she said quietly, "there is no reason to, even if we could. Our guests are safe and warm and perfectly content here at the mountain house. They aren't going anywhere."

"What about Kirk Rath?" Jill said.

Curt said, "He isn't going anywhere either."

Mary said, "It's not uncommon for us to be snow-bound here at Mohonk for several days. Par for the course, really."

I stood. Paced. "If the murderer is somebody here at the mountain house—one of the guest authors, for example, all of whom hated Rath—then he or she is stuck here, too."

"That's right," Mary said. Nodding sagely.

The phone rang again. Again it was for Mary.

Who spoke to Chief Colby for about five minutes, most of her contribution to the conversation being, "Uh-huh" and "Yes."

Then Colby asked to speak to me.

"Mr. Mallory," he said, "we may not be able to begin investigating for a while yet. You may have a murderer in that lodge somewhere. I'd suggest you keep what you know to yourself."

"Why?"

"To keep the murderer under that roof. Whoever it is, they don't know they've been found out yet. They don't know anybody's found the body. Let's keep it that way. Maybe when I *can* get my buggy up that mountain, we can catch the culprit flatfooted."

"I don't think it matters much either way," I said, not knowing what to make of a modern-day cop who used the word "culprit."

"Listen here. If that murderer finds out he's been found out, somebody *else* might get killed. Leave the damn lid on, okay?"

"Okay, Chief. I'll go along with you."

"Fine. Now, let me talk to Miss Wright again."

I did.

While she was talking to him, I explained to Curt and Jill that we were supposed to keep the murder under wraps, and why.

"I think that's a good idea," Jill said.

That response surprised me. "Why?"

"I'll tell you later."

Mary hung up and came over and managed to smile a little. "I'm glad we're agreed to keep quiet about this, for now. We can proceed with our weekend and not spoil anything for our guests."

"Except for Kirk Rath," Jill said. "The weekend's pretty well shot for him."

"You're drunk," Mary said nastily.

"Not drunk enough," Jill said. "When I look at you, you're still in focus."

They glared at each other for a while. Neither one seemed terribly well composed.

Curt was still working on his Scotch. He seemed vaguely amused. "Perhaps in the long run it will boost the Mystery Weekends, Mary. Think of the publicity."

"*Bad* publicity," she said, shaking her head, almost scowling.

"No such thing as," Curt affirmed, saluting her with his glass. Then he raised it in a more general toast: "And here's to Kirk Rath. God have mercy on him. Poor bastard."

I finished my Scotch.

But I was still cold inside.

Nevertheless, I was warmer than Kirk Rath, even if by now he was under a blanket.

12

• • •

Jill and I went back to our room and crashed for a while. We both felt unclean—the cold and snow hadn't kept us from working up a sweat hiking, and the lingering effect of finding a corpse had left a certain psychic film, a clammy residue over our minds, if not our bodies, that a shower wouldn't do much for, but we took one anyway. Together.

It wasn't a two-person orgy, so voyeurs in the audience can let loose of their expectations. In fact, it wasn't very sexual, really, or even romantic exactly. It *was* steamy, but only because we leaned on the hot water. We soaped each other's backs, massaged each other's tense neck muscles, clinging to each other a bit, nuzzling, but nothing more—just hurt animals licking each other's wounds. The shower stall provided a needed closeness, the fog of steam and the drilling of hot water on our bodies numbing us into something approaching relaxation, a melancholy mist we could get lost in for a while.

We shared a towel—conserving one for tomorrow morning—after which Jill slipped into her terrycloth robe, leaving me with the towel for a loincloth. She was rubbing her short black hair dry with a hand towel.

"I could build a fire," I said.

The wind was howling through the window.

"Let's save that for later," she said.

I sat next to her; the twin bed squeaked. "Why did you want me to go along with that bullshit about keeping the murder quiet?"

Her smile was one-sided and wry as she kept toweling her hair, looking at me sideways. "Surprised you, didn't it?"

"I should say. Especially since a man getting murdered seemed to upset Miss Wright primarily because her Mystery Weekend might get spoiled."

She kept toweling her hair. "The concealment wasn't Mary Wright's idea, though, was it?"

"No, it was that hick cop."

"How do you know he's a hick? Besides, this is New York; they don't have hicks in New York."

"Really? He used the word 'culprit' in a sentence."

"Oh dear. Well, I still think he was right, anyway."

"Why?"

She leaned her head back and shook her hair; droplets flew, and I blinked a couple away. "The murderer doesn't know that *we* know a murder has been committed," she said.

"So?"

"God, you're thick. And here you're supposed to be an amateur detective of sorts."

"Emphasis on the 'of sorts.' Anyway, there aren't any amateur detectives in real life."

She smiled flatly and shook her head again, not in an

effort to rid it of more water, though more droplets indeed flew, but in a gesture of amused frustration, as if from trying to reason with a slow child of whom you're rather fond.

"This *isn't* 'real life,' " she said. "It's Mohonk. More precisely, it's the Mohonk Mystery Weekend."

"Yeah, and Kirk Rath is really going all out in *his* role."

She ignored that and patted my bare leg. "Think of yourself as an unlicensed private eye," she said. "You figured out the circumstances of your friend Ginnie Mullens's murder, didn't you? I saw you in action, there; I know what you're capable of. So *do* it already—play unlicensed private eye again."

It was sinking in. "You mean, I could go around asking casual questions about Rath . . ."

She nodded eagerly; I liked the clean smell of her. "Yes, asking your various fellow 'suspects' in Curt's *Case of the Curious Critic* about their real-life relationships with Rath."

"And," I said, picking up on it, "get a reading on them, without the murderer among them knowing that I know a murder's even been committed."

"Exactly. With the exception of Curt Clark and Mary Wright, of course, who also know about the murder. And are also suspects."

I sighed, shrugged. "As far as I know, Mary Wright and Rath weren't even acquainted. And Curt's probably the only person here who *doesn't* have a motive to kill the critic. Besides, Curt's a tall drink of water, and the killer was a short, stocky person in a ski mask."

"Ah! The least likely suspect . . ."

"Oh, shut up. This is a real murder, not some stupid game."

That hurt her feelings a little; she glanced away and

started toweling her hair again, though it was pretty much dry by now.

"Sorry, kid," I said. "I know you're just as shaken by this goddamn thing as I am."

In a voice that seemed small for Jill Forrest, she said, "Maybe more. Maybe I never saw anything like that before."

I slipped my arm around her shoulder and she dropped the towel and we held each other; we weren't shaking, we weren't crying, but we did feel battered—or anyway I did. And, oddly, guilty. I told Jill as much.

"Why guilty?"

"Well," I said and sighed again, slipping out of her embrace and standing, adjusting my towel, "I didn't like the bum. I've said terrible things about the son of a bitch ... R.I.P. That makes me feel ... guilty, somehow, now that he's dead."

"You didn't *want* him dead."

"No." I shrugged, shook my head, and smiled without humor. "But I don't feel particularly *bad* that he's dead. I mean, the most I can muster is I feel kind of sorry for the guy. Jeez. That doesn't quite cut it, does it?"

Her mouth was a straight line, which turned into two straight lines as she said, "He was a smug, pompous, mean-spirited little jerk. And now he's a dead, smug, pompous, mean-spirited little jerk. Getting murdered doesn't make him a saint."

I went to the dresser and got out some fresh clothes. I dropped the towel and climbed into my shorts; when a man climbs into his shorts, it's very likely the moment that day he will feel the most vulnerable, the most mortal. Then putting the rest of his clothes on, a man begins to feel less like some dumb doomed animal. It's probably much the same for women. Getting into that outer skin of clothes, putting on the surface of civilization, applying the social veneer, creates a sense of order, taps into the security of ritual, makes us feel we're going to live forever. Or at least the rest of the day.

"I feel I owe Rath something," I said. "Maybe an apology. Or maybe to find his killer."

"Would you be surprised if I said I could understand that?"

I smiled at her; she smiled back, and it was as warm as the fire we'd almost made.

I said, "You're a constant surprise, as a matter of fact, but not in this instance. I've already picked up on your urge to play Nora to my Nick."

She laughed a little. "It always comes back to that—role playing, game playing. We *are* at Mohonk. No getting around it."

"And so is a murderer."

"So is a murderer."

I walked to the window; couldn't see much out of its frosted surface. The howl of the wind and snow kept finding its way through the cracks and crevices of the old hotel, a constant underpinning of all conversation, like an eerie score from an eerie movie.

Jill noticed it, too. "Maybe God put Bernard Herrmann in charge of the weather this weekend," she said.

I looked back at her, who still sat in her terry robe, hair dry now.

"We're well and truly snowbound," I said, "that's for sure. So we'll have this evening and most of tomorrow, unless I miss my guess, to do some casual investigating."

"Good," she said with a tight smile, fists in her lap.

"I will do the talking," I said, gesturing with a lecturing finger. "We have to be very careful. *Very* careful. If the murderer tips to what we're up to, we're in deep shit."

"Understood."

"I hope you do. Now get dressed and let's get something to eat. It's getting late, and they only serve till eight."

"How can you even *think* of eating?"

"Not only can I think of it," I said, coming over and taking her by one upper arm and pulling her up, "I can actually do it. Finding a dead body does take an edge off one's appetite, true. But hiking a couple of miles outweighs that, doesn't it? And besides, I haven't had a bite in over seven hours, and neither have you."

She was on her feet. "You're right. I *am* hungry."

And she threw on a shaggy gray sweater with wide shoulders and tugged on her black leather pants.

Soon we were sitting with Tom Sardini and Pete Christian among the dwindling diners in the huge dining room. Tom, in a cheery orange and white ski sweater over which he wore a "Miami Vice" white linen jacket (jackets were required for evening meals at Mohonk), was working on his dessert, a Linzer torte. Pete seemed restless, looking, in his rumpled brown suit and tie, as if he'd walked away unscathed from a building that had been demolished about him. But then he always did.

"My," Pete said, smiling, "you held out even longer than we did. I got in a conversation with some of the game-players and almost forgot to eat."

I wondered if Pete had noticed yet that we were snowbound; I didn't bother asking, though.

Jill said, "Is that kosher? Fraternization between suspects and players?"

"Sure!" Pete said, permitting that for all time with a wave of the hand. "You just have to watch them, that's all. Do you know the Arnolds?"

I was filling out my menu, circling my choices.

"Millie and Carl, you mean? Of the Casablanca Restaurant? Sure."

"Well, they can be devious," he said. He thumped a finger on the tablecloth. "You know, I wouldn't be a bit surprised if they proved to be the ones who staged that phony killing outside your window the other night."

"Somehow I doubt it," I said.

"Don't rule it out," Pete said, smiling, pushing his glasses up on his nose. "Millie has a theatrical background, and Carl's a karate expert. He could've staged some pretty convincing stunts on that snowy proscenium."

"Anything's possible," I said. A waiter came by and I handed him my filled-out menu and Jill's.

"Well, anyway, they were talking to me about my Charlie Chan movie book," Pete said, "and really got me going. Some subjects, if you get me started, it's like I've fallen off a cliff—I just don't stop till I hit bottom."

Jill was studying Pete; not too openly, I hoped. She said, "Why do you say the Arnolds can be devious?"

Pete's enthusiasm for life was contagious, and his laughter was too. "They were *studying* me, waiting for me to make a slip, a mistake, asking me to recount various plots of mystery films, wondering about the 'structure' of the mystery form. . . ."

"That sounds innocent enough," Jill said.

Tom pushed his plate away, clean. "You don't know Pete. If he saw a parallel between one of those stories and this weekend's mystery, he might blurt it out. Not thinking."

"Ah," Pete said, "but I'm always thinking. It's just that my enthusiasm gets in the way of my better judgment, at times."

"What role are you playing in *The Case of the Curious Critic*?" Jill asked him.

"I'm Rick Butler," Pete said, sitting up, proudly.

"Dapper man about town. Didn't you see me in my tux this morning?"

"Oh yes," Jill said, smiling. A waiter slipped a bowl of oxtail soup down in front of her. Me next.

"Curt's poking some fun at me," Pete said, smile settling in one corner of his mouth, "but I don't mind."

Tom was leaning back in his chair, grinning, gesturing at Pete with a thumb. "Curt turned Pete into a fashion plate."

"With a neatness fetish yet," Pete said. "You see before you a man who has now played *both* roles in *The Odd Couple*. My character also is an extremely fussy non-smoker. Allergic to cigarette smoke, to be exact. Whereas if I don't have a cigarette immediately, I'll begin throwing chairs." He stood and told Jill how charming she was and shambled off for his smoke.

"I like him," Jill said. "He has a gentlemanly manner."

"He's a nice man," I said. "But as much as he hates Kirk Rath, it's a little surprising he's here this weekend."

Tom shrugged. "Pete's just that kind of guy. He wouldn't let a louse like Rath spoil his weekend."

Jill was studying Tom, now. "Are you like everybody else around here?" she asked. "Did you hate Rath?"

"Rath or Sloth?" Tom asked.

Her past tense had confused him.

"Rath," she said, a little nervously, realizing her slip.

"I don't hate him exactly," Tom said. "He's cost me some money. I lost a series because of him."

"Really?" Jill said, surprised but trying not to show it. "TV?"

"Books," Tom said.

"What series was that?" I asked.

"That series I was going to do with a racetrack background. About a detective who worked for the racing commission?"

"Oh, yeah. . . . Didn't you do one of those?"

"Right. Only I was set to do two more till *The Mystery Chronicler* hung me out to dry."

Tom's bitterness had an edge to it, like the ice in the snow outside.

"What role do you play in Curt's mystery?" Jill asked. She was doing her best to seem casual; I could read her like a book, however, and like a book I wrote, at that. But maybe Tom couldn't.

"I'm Rob Darsini," he was saying, "A boxer turned private eye who is suspiciously like my character Jacob Miles. I was working for Sloth, it seems, but he tried to stiff me for my bill."

"Cost you money, in other words," Jill said. "Like in real life."

"Pete's character echoes real life, too," Tom said with a little shrug. "He mentioned it even touches on his having had a friend die by suicide after critic 'Sloth' trashed him—which is uncomfortably close to what happened to Pete's mentor C. J. Beaufort."

Jill seemed almost shocked. "Isn't it in rather bad taste of Curt to include such a thing?"

Tom laughed, but it was forced and a little weary. "Cute and nasty, that's our Curt. Though I think in fairness to him, it should be said it's Rath he meant to needle. I'm sure he's as disappointed as the rest of us that Rath split."

"Disappointed?" I said.

"Sure!" Tom said. "Weren't *you* hoping he'd hang around and be the murder victim? Don't we deserve that *vicarious* pleasure, at least?"

And he rose and said he'd see us later and left us to our supper.

13

. . .

The entertainment for the evening was Peter Christian's Charlie Chan movie marathon—three flicks preceded by an informative but not at all dry slide show, with Pete regaling the attentive crowd in the Parlor with anecdotes and little-known facts while flashing onto the screen rare stills, movie posters, and candid shots of the various movie Chans, as well as photos of the oriental detective's creator, Earl Derr Biggers, and dustjackets of first editions and early paperbacks. From George K. Kuwa, the screen's first Chan (in an abbreviated appearance in a 1926 silent), to the relatively recent (and disastrous) Peter Ustinov-starring-as-Chan film, it was all there.

And, as a mystery buff and late show devotee from way back, I was enjoying myself; but for my investigative purposes the evening's entertainment was a bigger disaster than the Ustinov movie. Tomorrow night a dance was scheduled in this time slot, which would be ideal for mingling and casual questioning; however, this was tonight, and movies. In most Charlie Chan films, there is a scene in which all the suspects are gathered in one room and, suddenly, somebody turns out the lights! The situation tonight was similar—all the suspects were gathered here, in this mammoth hall, but the lights were already out. And, unlike a Chan film, where the lights would be out but for a moment, this would be a four-hour haul. In the dark.

Out of courtesy to Pete (and because his presentation was plenty of fun, even for somebody as preoccupied as I was), I sat through the slide show; movie nut Jill insisted on sitting through *Charlie Chan at the Opera*, during which she bet me a million dollars I didn't know who wrote the opera Boris Karloff and the others were singing. I won the bet. It was Oscar Levant, and Jill still hasn't paid up.

When *Charlie Chan at Treasure Island* started unfolding, Jill grabbed my arm and whispered. "This is my favorite one. I *have* to see it."

"What happened to playing Nora to my Nick?"

"All your suspects are watching the movies," she whispered.

"Culver isn't here."

"He was."

"Well, he ducked out in the last reel of the *Opera*."

"How *could* he?"

"It was easy." I thought for a moment. "You know, this might be a good chance for me to get him alone."

Cynthia Crystal hadn't left; she was sitting with Jack Flint and his wife, drinking in Sidney Toler's finest Chan.

"I'm watching the movie," Jill said. "It's only an hour. See you at the room, after?"

"What about the next Chan up?"

"It's a Roland Winters. I like it okay, but enough's enough."

"I'm glad to hear you say that. I don't know if I want to hang around with a woman who'd sit through *three* Charlie Chan movies."

Somebody in the row in front of us turned and said, angrily, "Shusssh!" Quite rightly, too—generally I feel people who talk during movies should be shot.

Feeling guilty for violating one of my own rules, I rolled my fingers at Jill in a Stooges wave and slinked out of the Parlor.

I went to Culver's room, which was just a few doors down from ours, and knocked. No answer.

So I began exploring the mountain house, wandering its endless halls, occasionally finding little covens of Mystery Weekenders, who were playing hookey from the night's entertainment to keep working on their solution to *The Case of the Curious Critic*. Since a number of the gamesters were puzzle fanatics as opposed to mystery fans, their absence from the Chan festival, and their obsession with working on the puzzle, made sense. Using "sense" loosely.

Anyway, they were here and there, in the little sitting rooms with the plush furnishings and the fireplaces, many of which were going now, the snow piling up outside the frosted-over windows. Strangely, I'd heard no one complain about being stranded. Perhaps that was because all of us were, in a manner of speaking, stranded here already, and of our own free will. Being snowbound merely added to the atmosphere, whether *Ten Little Indians*—Agatha Christie or *Shining*—Stephen King.

I should have been depressed, I supposed. A man had died; I'd seen him killed one day, and found his body the next. That I had done both seemed wildly coincidental to me, certainly nothing I'd try to get away with in one of my books. But it had happened, so what was I supposed to do about it? You can start over in fiction; in life you're stuck with what you're dealt.

But I felt a certain charge out of the situation—being snowbound, having a chance to try to find out "whodunit" before the police got here (tomorrow or Sunday or Monday or whenever the hell snow and fate allowed), having one up on the murderer by knowing about the murder when he or she thought it had gone as yet undetected and, well, it was exciting. I was like any other Mohonk game-player—I enjoyed the challenge, and I wanted to solve the puzzle.

At the same time my more rational self was cautioning me not to consider this a game; to remember the ghastly slashed face of Rath (as if I could forget) and to keep in mind that the person I was pursuing had committed that violent crime. It might be a Christie situation, but some King-style violence was in the air.

I discovered the big-screen TV room, finally; the monstrous thing was shut off, the chairs before it empty—Pete's Chan show was getting the ratings tonight. Next I ran across a cement-floored game room, tucked away at the end of one hall like a poor relation, where pinballs and video games were being played by young off-duty employees, and a Yuppie-ish young couple was playing pool. No sign of Culver, but the pool-playing Yuppies were my new friends, Jenny and Frank Logan. They were just racking up for another game when they noticed me.

"Oh!" Jenny said. She wore a green sweater and gray slacks and filled them out nicely, thank you. "We'd been hoping to run into you. And this makes a good out-of-the-way place to talk."

It was; the game room was dark and dingy and was very much like most of the bars back in Port City, only

I didn't notice anybody serving beer, let alone hard stuff.

"This must be where the Quakers go to go nuts," I said.

"We've got our own little bar back in our room," Jenny said.

"But," Frank warned, beige cardigan, pale blue shirt, gray slacks, "we're liable to be interrupted by our fellow team players."

Jenny smirked in a good-humored way. "We're sort of hiding out from them."

"Why?" I asked.

"They want to keep hashing and rehashing the interrogation info," she said.

"I thought you two took this stuff pretty seriously."

"Sure," Frank said, "but we don't go overboard."

"Besides," Jenny said with a smug little smile, "we know who did it."

"Oh?"

"And," she went on, "we won't be working on the creative aspects of our presentation till tomorrow, so what the hell. Let's live a little."

I glanced around the game room. "If you call this living."

"We've spent hours today in one little hotel room," she said, heaving a theatrical sigh, "huddled with our fellow game-players. Just had to get away."

"So you know who did it?" I said. Amused in spite of myself.

"Sure," she said, grinning. "You."

And they looked at me. Watched me. Even, one might say, studied me.

Finally I said, "Am I expected to confirm that or deny it or something?"

They shrugged, wearing smirky smiles.

"You guys are real cute," I said, and took up a pool

cue and broke their balls. I started shooting around the table, not playing any game, just randomly sinking the balls, missing now and then.

"Can't blame a girl for trying," Jenny said, sidling up next to me. She was wearing Giorgio perfume; I'm no expert, but I recognized it as what Jill wears. The combination of being reminded of jealous Jill, and Jenny's husband lurking nearby, kept me from letting my thoughts run wild. But it did occur to me, for a fleeting, frightening instant, that Frank might let me sleep with his wife if I'd tell them what I knew about the nonexistent Sloth murder.

Jenny said, "We asked around for you."

"Oh," I said. "That's great." I didn't know how to tell them that their efforts had been pointless. I wasn't about to let them know I'd established that the "prank" had been real, via finding the very real corpse.

Frank sidled up on the other side of me; he smelled like English Leather. I used to use it. Now I wear nothing at all.

Frank said, "We think maybe the Arnolds pulled that stunt."

"The Casablanca restaurant couple?"

"Yes. She used to be an actress, and he's—"

"A karate expert," I said. "Yeah, I know."

Jenny said, "Have you talked to them yet?"

"No, uh . . . but I will."

Frank moved away, leaned over the table and banked the eight ball into a corner pocket. "They seem to be the only group this year," he said, "that brought along fairly elaborate theatrical gear."

"That we know of for sure," she added. "There are at least half a dozen theater pros here, and some of them may have brought along more stuff than they were willing to cop to, to the 'enemy.' "

I put the pool cue away. I liked these people, but they

were too attractive and smelled to
comfortable around them.

"Thanks for checking," I said. "Yo
anything more."

"It was fun," Jenny said. "We fel
spies."

Frank slipped his arm around her wa we still
think you did it," he said.

"No comment," I said. "How do you like being
snowbound?"

"I think it's cool," Jenny said, beaming.

An understatement worthy of Hammett.

They went back to playing pool and hiding out, and
I walked out into the hall. I was nearing our room when
somebody called out to me.

"Excuse me!"

I turned and looked.

It was the intense young man with glasses who'd
been so dogged in his questioning at the interrogation
this morning; he was wearing the same gray sweater,
and the same pained expression.

"Mr. Mallory," he said. "A moment of your time,
please."

It was the kind of politeness that respects social ritual
but not you. His words were bullets, fired in a rush at
me, and they fairly dripped dislike.

"I don't believe we've met," I said.

His hair was short and mouse-colored, and the eyes
behind the thick glasses were as gray as his sweater and
bore dark circles and red fillagree. He would have been
a bigger nerd than Lester Denton, except he seemed
muscular, if a head shorter than me, and the veins stood
out in his hands. That is, his fists. Clenched fists,
actually—it may seem redundant to describe a fist as
"clenched," but not if you saw these fists.

"I'm Rick Fahy," he said.

to be confused with Rick Butler, Pete's character the weekend mystery, of course.

"Pleased to meet you," I said. I guessed. I extended a hand for him to shake. He thought about it, unclenched his right hand, and we shook. His grip was a vise and my fingers were so many toothpaste tubes to be squeezed.

I pulled back my hand; I could feel my pulse five times in it.

"Okay," I said. "So you work out. I'm impressed. Who the hell are you?"

"I told you. I'm Rick Fahy. Has something happened to Rath?"

That stopped me. I rolled Fahy's name around in my brain and gathered who he was.

"I know you," I said, pointing at him. "You're with *The Mystery Chronicler.*"

"That's right," he said.

"You're up here covering the weekend for your magazine."

"Yes."

"A piece from the perspective of someone who's been here and played the game."

"Yes. Has something happened to Rath?"

"Not that I know of," I lied. "Why?"

He looked at me hard; his mouth was a thin pale line. A vein throbbed in his forehead. The skin around his eyes was crinkly, like Charles Bronson deciding who to kill. Was I about to get the crap beaten out of me by a *Chronicler* intellectual? And if so, *why* the hell?

"I asked you this morning," he said, carefully; the bullets firing more slowly now, "if you saw something out your window last night."

"Actually," I said, "you asked Lester Denton if he'd seen Roark K. Sloth killed outside his, that is, *Denton's*, window last night."

"I don't like smart-asses."

"I don't like threats."

He thought about that; he tasted whatever was in his mouth at the time. Baskins Robbins Flavor of the Moment, perhaps.

Then he said, "Did you see Rath outside your window last night?"

This time I thought before responding. Then I told him what I'd seen, ending with, "But whether it was Rath or not, I couldn't say. Maybe it was—I thought at the *time* it was—but I understand there are plenty of players here with theatrical training, and makeup kits and props and such along with them."

"I've tried to call Rath."

"So have I," I said, "and I haven't had any luck."

He looked at me like I was a slug; then he looked away. He sighed. There was frustration in it, and anger, too.

I said, "If you're a friend of Rath's—"

"He's my employer. And he's missing."

"Did you know he was going to stalk out like that Thursday? Refuse to play the weekend game?"

Fahy's lip curled ever so slightly; it wasn't a sneer exactly—it seemed to correspond with him thinking, deciding whether or not to answer me.

He decided.

Not to.

He walked away and I watched him go, and shrugged, and went into the room.

Where I found Jill sitting before a roaring fire, a blanket wrapped around her like an Indian chief.

"What happened to Charlie Chan?"

"I watched half an hour," she said. "Then my mind started to wander ... thinking about the murder and all."

"Ah." I pulled my sweater off.

"Come sit with me."

I stripped off the rest of my clothes, and did. It was cold outside, the windows rattling, wind whistling, snow piling up, but it was toasty warm in here, two naked peopled in a blanket before a fire.

"You should've let me build this," I said, rubbing my hands, basking in the orange glow and the warmth.

"You build a truly pathetic fire," she said.

"I do not!"

"But you do."

"Well. I suppose."

"The really good fires, back in Iowa, have been the ones *I* started."

"This is true," I admitted. She was starting a sort of fire right now, as a matter of fact.

"Did you find Culver?" she asked.

"No," I said.

"Did you talk to anybody?"

"Yes," I said.

"Who?"

"Later," I said, and kissed her.

And then I kissed her again.

"Nick . . ."

"Yes, Nora?"

"Let's do what married people do."

And we did. Maybe we didn't have the river view from my little house in Port City, Iowa, but we did have the fire, the blanket, and each other. And we sure didn't give a damn about anything else.

For the moment.

PART THREE

...

Saturday

14

. . .

I woke up rested, but aching. Yesterday had been a long day, and despite everything I had on my mind, I slept soundly. Nobody at Mohonk, save possibly Kirk Rath himself, could have had a deeper night's sleep. I had no memory of having dreamed, so apparently my exhaustion had kept me from pursuing Rath's killer through slumberland. But the mountain hike in the real world had taken its toll: muscles I didn't know I had made their acquaintance by twanging like painfully out-of-tune guitar strings whenever, wherever I moved.

Jill was again showering—it was a wonder she didn't go all pruney, as many showers as she took—and I stumbled into the john and took an unceremonious pee. I brushed my teeth and splashed some water on my face and pretty soon Jill came out, wrapping her slim, tan, water-beaded body in a towel (a body whose attributes I noted only with clinical interest, because anything more than thought would have twanged too many painful guitar strings) and bequeathed the shower to me.

Five hot minutes later, I was refreshed, awake, still hurting, but also thinking. The Rath murder had hold of me and it wasn't going to let me go till I did something about it.

Jill sat in her terrycloth robe, doing her makeup at the dresser. "How are you feeling today, Nick?"

"Couldn't be better, Nora. Unless I could trade this tired old body in for a new one."

"I like your body just fine."

"My body isn't interested. Not until it gets some aspirin, anyway. What's the situation outside?"

"Still snowing."

"You're kidding! Hasn't let up?"

"Well, if it did, it started back up again."

I went to the window and rubbed a place to look out. The snow was piled up just past the sill. The white stuff was indeed still coming down, however rather lazily now—just dusting the drifts. The blizzard was over, apparently, but its aftermath would take an army of snowplows.

"It'll be a miracle if the cops get up here today," I said, climbing into my shorts.

Jill was stepping into some loose-fitting gray slacks. "Looks like we're still in the detective business."

Her remark made my enthusiasm for the real-life *Curious Critic* case wilt like the ardor of a bridegroom whose mother-in-law showed up at the honeymoon.

I finished dressing and went over to her. "We have to talk. Sit down for a minute."

She did, on the edge of the bed, looking at me curiously.

I sat next to her, put my hands on her shoulders, and stared her right in those cornflower-blue eyes that had helped make me fall so hard for her.

I said, "I think maybe we should forget about the Nick and Nora bit. I think maybe we should wait for the police like everybody else, even if it does take till tomorrow."

"Nobody's waiting for the police except you and me and Mary Wright and Curt Clark."

"Don't get technical. You saw that body."

She didn't say anything.

"You *saw* that body," I said.

She looked away.

"Look at me, Jill. Look at me!"

She looked, but her mouth was twisted up a bit.

"You saw that body," I said. "You saw the way Rath was killed."

She sucked in some breath; then, slowly, she let it out, nodding as she did, nodding several times.

"You get my drift? And I'm not talking about the weather."

"I get your drift," she said. "There's a murderer among us." The latter was delivered rather archly.

My hands were still on her shoulders. I squeezed. "There *is* a murderer among us. Somebody vicious. Rath's body wasn't the result of a scuffle that got out of hand or something. That was a savage goddamn *murder*—a bloody, psychopathic job of one, too, I'd say."

"So we should just wait for the police," she said, "to sort it all out."

I took my hands off her shoulders. "Yes. In the cool clear light of day, that's how I see it."

"It's not cool, it's cold, and if there's any clear light out there, you'll freeze your butt off in it."

"Agreed. But do you get my point?"

"I get your point. I get your drift."

She rose. Walked to the door.

"It's quarter till nine," she said, indifferently. "They only serve breakfast till nine. Shake a leg."

In my condition, shaking a leg was out of the question, but I did follow her, down the hall, and I do mean follow. She was walking quickly. I couldn't keep up with her at first. Finally I caught up, grabbing her arm, gently but firmly, stopping her.

"Why are you angry?"

She pouted. "Because you're no fun."

"I'm no fun."

She smirked in a one-sided, humorless fashion. "That's not it, really. It's that you're ... well ... shit. It's that you're *right*."

I smiled at her, just a little. "I can't help it. I just don't want you or me, singly or together, to do anything that will put you—or us—in any danger. Which if we keep nosing around, we will be."

She nodded, faintly amused, overtly disappointed, hooked her arm in mine, and we walked up the stairs and down the hall to the big dining room.

Which at this hour was damn near empty.

Instead of sitting at our own table, we went to the adjacent one, where Curt and the rest of the guests usually sat. Curt wasn't there, however—the only person left at the fairly large table was Cynthia Crystal, who sat drinking a cup of coffee, gazing into not much of anything.

"You mind if we join you?" I asked.

Cynthia's trance broke, and she smiled in her elegant, crinkly fashion. She was dressed in designer jeans and a red MURDER INK sweatshirt, which was as casual as I'd ever seen her; but she still looked like a million dollars. Two.

"Do please join me," she said, gesturing to a chair on either side of her.

We took our places, and a waiter came over and I asked him if we were too late for breakfast, and he said, "Not at all," even though we were. Jill and I quickly circled our chosen items on the little green gazebo-crested menus, and passed them along to him.

"Tim's out jogging," Cynthia said. "He jogs every morning without fail."

"In *that*?" I said, pointing, vaguely, toward the Great White Out-of-Doors.

"No, dear," she said with a brief brittle laugh, "he's running the halls on the upper floors. My Tim is eccentric, but no fool."

"You know, Cynthia," I said, carefully, "the last time I saw you, you and Tim seemed, well . . ."

"On the verge of the abyss, where our relationship was concerned? Ah, yes. But we've retreated to the sunny countryside of connubial bliss. Which is to say, now we're planning to get married. Make it official."

"No kidding! Congratulations."

I offered her my hand to shake, but she took her head and smiled in near embarrassment, as if to say, *How gauche*, and turned her cheek for me to kiss. Which I did.

Jill congratulated Cynthia as well, asking "How did you manage to go from nearly splitting up, to about to tie the knot? If I'm not prying."

"Oh you *are* prying," Cynthia said, without malice, smiling rather regally, "but as a gossip myself, I don't mind at all. Fact is, Tim . . . and Mal knows all about this . . . was rather jealous of me."

Jill narrowed her eyes, tilted her head, not understanding.

Cynthia clarified: "Not of my ability to charm the . . . socks off the likes of young Mallory, here . . . nothing so sexy as that. Well, you tell her, Mal. My modesty prevents me."

"Your modesty," I said to Cynthia, "wouldn't prevent much of anything. But in fact," I continued, directing this to Jill, "Cynthia's had a good deal of success in re-

cent years. And while Tim's always been a critical darling, his books have never sold very well. He's bounced
from publisher to publisher, never taking hold."

Jill was nodding—our earlier conversation with Cynthia coming back—saying, "Whereas his brother Curt's
done well both in book sales and with all those movies."

"Precisely," Cynthia said, precisely. "So God bless
Kirk Rath."

"And Lawrence Kasdan," Jill put in.

The waiter put my orange juice down in front of me.
I sipped it, then said, "Then the combination of Tim's
movie sale and Curt's favorable *Chronicler* reviews not
only got Tim and his brother Curt back on speaking
terms, but—"

"But helped Tim overcome his career jealousy of me,
as well, yes," she said. "Thanks to that little weasel
Rath."

Her praise for the critic surprised me, even if it was
lefthanded. "I sensed Thursday night there was no love
lost between Rath and Tim," I said. "Tim seemed about
an inch away from pounding Rath into jelly, for getting
rude with you."

"Tim despises Rath," Cynthia said, lightly.

"But I saw two major articles on Tim in the *Chronicler*, and even an interview . . ."

"Yes," Cynthia said, "but remember—Tim's never
been lacking for critical praise. That's *typical* of Rath,
the little dilettante, giving favorable reviews to someone
who's safely singled out already by other, more astute,
critics."

"Still," Jill said, "why dislike somebody who praises
your work, whatever the reason? It seems like plenty of
people have been burned by Rath. . . . Shouldn't your
fiancé be relieved, at least, that Rath's never attacked
him?"

"Fiancé," Cynthia said, rolling it around. "That has a nice sound, doesn't it?"

She was ducking the issue.

"Weren't Rath and Tim rather close, at one time?" I asked.

"Yes we were, Mr. Mallory," Tim Culver said.

He had come up behind us. Like his brother, whom he resembled just enough to make it spooky, he was a big, lean man; he was wearing another lumberjack plaid shirt and jeans. He was polishing his wire-rim glasses with a napkin from a nearby table and his expression was solemn and not particularly friendly.

I stood. "Please call me Mal, if you would. And I apologize for prying."

"No problem," he said, though it clearly was. He sat next to his fiancée, in the chair I'd warmed, and I moved to the other side of Jill.

Who rushed in where Mallory feared to tread, saying, "We were just wondering why you would dislike somebody who gave you so much favorable press. Rath, that is."

Culver sighed; pressed his lips together. Turned inward even more, to consider whether or not to address this subject.

Then he called a waiter over and said, "Breakfast?"

"Certainly, sir," the waiter said, and Culver put his glasses back on and quickly marked a menu and handed it along.

Then Culver looked past his fiancée and Jill, toward me, and said, "I blame myself."

Culver intimidated me a little, so I said nothing.

Jill doesn't intimidate worth a damn, and said, "Blame yourself for what?"

Another heavy sigh. "For being ... seduced." The latter was spoken with quiet but distinct sarcasm.

"How so?" Jill asked.

"Rath's praise was so effusive, it took me in."

"Was it?" Jill said, continuing to prompt him. Culver spoke in telegrams.

"I'd never had that kind of praise before."

I finally got the nerve to get in the act. "Tim—if you don't mind my calling you that—you've had nothing but praise from critics since the day you published your first novel. . . ."

Culver shook his head slowly, twice. "Not that kind of praise."

"Oh," I said. "You mean, the mystery-fandom-goes-to-graduate-school sort of praise you got in the *Chronicler*. High-fallutin', pretentious, toney-type praise. You and Hemingway and Faulkner and Hammett all in the same sentence."

"Yeah," Culver said, disgusted with himself.

"So," Cynthia said, being cautious not to step on her lover's reticent toes, "Tim agreed to be interviewed."

"I *never* give interviews," Culver said, sneering faintly. "I'm like Garbo: leave me the hell alone."

"But you gave Rath an interview," Jill said.

"Yes," Culver said.

"Why?" Jill asked.

He pounded the table with one fist; silverware jumped. "I *said* why. The little bastard flattered me into it."

Silence.

The waiter brought Jill her poached eggs and me my corned beef hash and Culver some coffee, refilling Cynthia's cup as well.

Then Culver said, "I'd been drinking. They flattered me, and *we* began drinking, moved from bar to hotel room like so many seductions and then I said, 'Sure. I'll do an interview.' "

Cynthia smiled nervously. "Tim does loosen up a bit

when he drinks. Christ, I wish you could smoke in here."

Tim said, "I talked too much. I said things I shouldn't have."

"Such as?"

Tim drank some coffee. "I said insulting things about another writer."

I leaned forward, squinting at him, as if that would make me see inside him better. "You're not involved in one of Rath's libel suits, are you . . . ?"

"No! I wish to God I were." He leaned an elbow on the table and covered his eyes with the thumb and third finger of his right hand.

When he took the hand away, his eyes were red and a little wet. He said, "I said awful things about C. J. Beaufort."

"Oh," I said. Pete Christian's friend and mentor, the one who'd committed suicide not long ago, after several years of ridicule in the *Chronicler.*

"I had nothing against Beaufort or his work," he said. "I've probably not read more than a short story or two of his, over the years. But we were drinking, and Rath and his crony started laughing about the 'King of the Hacks. . . .' "

Cynthia, one of whose hands rested on Culver's nearest one, said quietly, "It grew out of a discussion of Tim's working methods—out of the fact that Tim publishes only one book a year, a finely polished piece of work, unlike many others in the business—like your friend Sardini, say, who fairly churns them out."

"You have to make a living," I said, in defense of those writers. "And some, like Tom, write very well."

"I know," Culver said. "Perhaps I resent the likes of Sardini . . . and Beaufort. I had to supplement my writing career with a teaching job. They make a living from their words alone. But, hell—I had nothing against

Beaufort. If I'd been given the opportunity to edit my interview, as I'd been promised, the references to Beaufort would've been deleted. I'd have been sober, then. Goddamn—I never even met Beaufort." He shook his head, his mouth tight with self-disgust. "And the poor son of a bitch blew his brains out over a copy of the *Chronicler.* Opened to my interview."

The only sound in the high-ceilinged hall was the clink of a dish and the wind-rattle of the windows.

I said, "You can hardly hold yourself responsible...."

Culver looked at me with eyes like glowing coals and thumped his chest with a thick forefinger. "I hold myself responsible for *every* thing I do, *every* word I speak. And I have no respect for any man who doesn't."

I swallowed. "That's a pretty charitable outlook."

Culver scowled at me, and then looked away, and raised his coffee cup to his lips and drank.

Jill, not knowing when to leave bad enough alone, said, "Why in God's name did you agree to come here, then? If Rath was going to be here?"

Culver put the coffee cup down. "Because my brother asked me."

Jill still didn't get it. "If your brother knew about the bitterness between you and Rath, then why would he impose on you so?"

If I'd asked him that, he might have smacked me; but his Hammett-like code included a certain surface chivalry toward the ladies.

He said, "My brother doesn't know how deep my bitterness runs. We've never discussed the subject of Rath."

"Besides," Cynthia said lightly, her smile forced, "what could Tim say to the invitation but yes? He and Curt had just, well, patched things up after being estranged for so long ... he could hardly refuse him.

And, besides, who could be mad at Curt for inviting Rath? It was the natural thing for him to do."

"Why?" I asked. "Because Rath always praised Curt in the *Chronicler*?"

"That," Cynthia said, "and, of course, they go back a very long way."

That was news to me. I said so.

"Oh, they go back *ages*," she said, as if everybody knew that. "Curt's son Gary was Kirk's roommate when they were college kids at NYU."

"It's the first I heard of it."

Culver spoke, reluctantly. "That's part of why I allowed Rath to sucker me. He was like one of Curt's family."

"Or anyway, he was back in those days," Cynthia added. "I think it was meeting Curt that turned the young Kirk Rath on to mystery fiction in the first place."

"And with Gary gone, now," Culver said, "my brother feels a bond to that little bastard." He meant Rath. "So I wasn't about to bring up my feelings about Rath, not with Curt still so broke up."

"About the loss of his son, you mean," I said.

Culver nodded. Then he shrugged facially. "I guess it's like old home week for Curt."

"How's that?" I asked.

Culver shrugged his shoulders. "That social director here, what's her name? She's the one that booked Curt in to do this Mystery Weekend."

"Mary Wright, you mean?"

"Yeah. Mary Wright. She was thick with both of them."

"Both of who?"

"Kirk and Gary. She went with Gary, for a while, I think, back at NYU. They were schoolmates there, the three of them."

15
...

Jack Flint was giving a talk, which he'd begun at ten o'clock, on the differences between real-life private-eyes and fictional ones. I would have loved to hear it, under other circumstances; but what I was there for was Mary Wright, who I found standing in the back of the Parlor, in her blue Mohonk blazer, clipboard in hand.

I had asked Jill to wait in our room; I knew she didn't like Mary Wright, and I knew Mary Wright didn't like her. So I figured I might get further with the Mohonk social director, alone.

"Could I have a few minutes of your time?" I asked her.

She looked at me gravely, dark brown eyes narrowing; as one of the handful who knew about the Rath murder, all I meant to her was bad news. Any inclination to flirt with me was long gone, now.

"Is something wrong?" she whispered.

"Everything's peachy. Where can we talk privately?"

We went to her small office on the ground floor; she sat behind the desk and fussed with some artificial flowers in a vase as we spoke. A framed print of kittens playing with a ball of yarn hung on the wall nearby. I sat across from her.

"Yes, I knew Kirk Rath," she said. "Did I ever say I didn't?"

"No. But it does seem relevant."

"Does it?"

"I think so. Why didn't you mention it?"

"Why should I? Is it so surprising? Did you suppose I arranged weekends like these by placing my finger on some random name in the phone book? Of course I call upon people I know."

"Then it was *you* who invited Rath here."

"I suggested him to Curt, when I first invited Curt to do the Mystery Weekend. He was reluctant at first. . . ."

"To invite Rath?"

She shook her head, mildly irritated. "No, to take over planning the Mystery Weekend. You see, previously we had Don Westlake, and Curt was reluctant to follow in Don's footsteps."

I understood that; Curt worked the same literary territory as Westlake but had always played second fiddle to him with the reviewers.

"But then he said yes," she said, "after I told him some of my ideas."

"One of which was to have Rath as a murder victim."

"Well, to invite him, anyway, yes, that was my idea. You know what a wicked sense of humor Curt has, and Kirk was certainly a controversial figure. I thought it would be . . . fun."

"It has been a million laughs, hasn't it?"

She said nothing, frowning, fiddling with the artificial flowers.

"You didn't—and don't—seem too broken up about the death of your old friend, now do you?"

She shrugged, her mouth tightening; then she said, "We were never close. Just acquaintances. We went to school together, college I mean, ran with the same bunch."

"Specifically, Curt's son."

She frowned. "Yes. Gary was a mutual friend."

"He was your boyfriend, wasn't he?"

"Gary?" Now she smiled, but there was sadness in it. "We were just friends."

"Didn't you go together?"

"Briefly. We tried to make it work. Look, Mr. Mallory, this is getting a little personal."

"As opposed to something as detached as murder."

She sat up; looked at me pointedly. "Kirk Rath is dead, and I'm sorry, but there can be little doubt that the mean-spirited way he treated people got him killed."

"I hate it when a critic pans me," I said, "but I never killed one for it. I don't know of any instance in the history of man where a critic got killed by his unhappy subject."

"Maybe you don't know your history," she said coldly, looking away from me now, playing with the flowers again.

"Or history maybe got made here," I said.

"Is that all? I'm a busy woman."

"Ah yes. You have a weekend to run. Answer my question, and I'll go."

"What question?"

"I guess I never got around to asking it. Why did you and Gary break up?"

She sighed, straining for patience, looking at me with mock-pity and genuine condescension. "Gary was gay, Mr. Mallory."

"Oh."

"He didn't know it, or didn't admit it to himself, till college. He tried to be straight. Wanted to. We were friends ... we tried to make something more of it. It just didn't work out."

"I see."

"Now, if you're quite through prying into my personal life, could I ask you to leave? I believe you have a role to play in just a few minutes. ..."

She was right; at eleven-thirty, to be exact. This was Saturday morning, which marked the second and final interrogation of suspects in *The Case of the Curious Critic*, just half an hour from now. I excused myself, and she wasn't sorry to see me go. I went to the room, reported Mary Wright's revelations to Jill, who said nothing, just mulled them over as she helped me get ready, as once again I nerded myself up to be Lester Denton—pencil mustache, Brylcream, window-glass glasses, black-and-red-and-white plaid corduroy suit and all.

But my heart was not in it, as I again sat in the little open parlor, with the cold frosted windows to my back and a roaring fireplace to my left, and a new batch of eager Mystery Weekenders all around, all but grilling me over that open fire.

The teams had divided their memberships up differently, so that no player would interrogate the same suspect twice—with one notable exception: Rick Fahy was again in the audience, in a front row seat, in fact. Today he wore a green sweater and blue jeans, but his expression remained pained, and the gray eyes behind the thick glasses were still red-veined and dark-circled. He looked like hell.

Only today he didn't ask a single question; his Hamilton Burger routine at yesterday's interrogation—and the one conducted in earnest in last night's encounter in the hall, for that matter—was conspicuously absent. He just sat staring at me with haunted eyes, unnerving me.

Jill was in the audience too, in the back, leaning against a support beam, getting her first look at Lester Denton in action.

Taking Jenny and Frank Logan's places in the Overenthusiastic Yuppie Division were the fabled Arnolds, Millie and Carl. Millie—a slim little bubbly redheaded woman with attractive, angular features—was the interrogator, while her dark, mustached husband—a small man behind whose mild demeanor lurked a black belt in Karate—sat taking the notes. They both wore ski sweaters and jeans, and sat forward, hanging on Lester's every word.

"Are you aware that Sloth had published a vicious review of his own *grandmother's* first mystery novel?" Millie said, her words rushing out. All of Millie's words came rushing out.

"No," I said. I was aware, however, that the grandmother role was being played by Cynthia Crystal.

"And that upon reading the review," Millie continued, "she had a heart attack?"

"No," I said. None of this was on my Suspect sheet; they were wasting their time going down this alley. But what the hell, it was their time.

Another player—a heavy-set woman of about forty, dressed all in dark blue—gestured with her pen and said, "Sloth's grandmother was seen going to his room shortly before you did. Did *you* see her?"

"No," I said, meekly. "But I'm most relieved to hear the dear lady made a full recovery."

"Then you weren't aware," Millie said, "that Sloth hired a thief to break into his grandmother's house, to see if she'd changed her will, in the aftermath of that review?"

"No," I said. All I knew of this aspect of Curt's mystery was that Tim Culver was playing the thief.

Carl Arnold spoke; his deadpan expression barely cracked as he said, "Did Sloth say anything about his grandmother when you saw him?"

"No," I said.

"He said nothing about a bribe?" Millie pressed.

"Well . . ."

"Did he say anything about a bribe? Specifically, that he told his grandmother he'd review her next book favorably, if she put him back in the will?"

"I knew nothing of that," I said.

Another of the players, another Yuppie male in a white cardigan and pale blue shirt, picked up on my reaction to the word "bribe" and said, "You have a wealthy background, don't you, Mr. Denton?"

"Well, I wouldn't say 'wealthy' . . ."

"What *would* you say?"

"Mother is well-fixed."

"Did you offer money to Sloth that night?"

"Well, uh . . ."

"*Did* you, Mr. Denton?"

Whereupon I broke down and confessed having attempted to bribe Roark K. Sloth; I further confessed to his having laughed off my "pathetic" attempt to do so.

Millie Arnold's eyes were glittering; she smelled blood, and it put a great big smile right under her nose. "Did Sloth threaten you with a tape recording?"

"Y-yes," Lester and I said. "He had recorded our entire conversation on a pocket machine."

Soon the interrogation was over; I'd done an all right job—not as good as the first time around, but the first time around I had only a probable prank on my mind, not a real live murder. Still, a number of the interrogators hung around to compliment me and chat and laugh a little. They were having a great time, the players were; this was the best Mystery Weekend yet, several veterans said.

Among the lingerers were the Arnolds. Millie approached me and asked if she could give Lester a kiss; I said sure and she bussed Lester's cheek.

"You were *great*," she said, slapping me on the shoulder. I wasn't great. She was just enthusiastic.

Jill wandered up and I made introductions all around.

"You seemed pleased to get that piece of business about the tape," I said to Millie and Carl, making polite conversation.

"Oh, yes—that helps us confirm a suspicion. Sloth tape-recorded everybody—Tom Sardini's private-eye character has admitted to helping Sloth go so far as to wiretap."

"Also," Carl added, "Jack Flint's character admitted to being threatened with a blackmail tape . . . but no tapes were found in Sloth's room."

"I see," I said, not really giving a damn.

"Could I ask you a question?" Millie said, which was a question itself, actually.

"Sure," I said.

"Did you send Jenny Logan around to check up on us? We figured she was trying to find out if we pulled that stunt outside your window. Because we brought our theatrical gear along and all."

"Actually, I did ask her to check around."

"Then you weren't in on it?" Carl said.

"In on what?"

"The stunt," Millie said. "We figured it was a part of the Mystery Weekend—something Curt Clark cooked up. Most of the teams are working it into their solutions."

"Then they're going down the wrong road," I said. "The mystery is strictly limited to the information you gather from the interrogation sessions—nothing else before or after counts."

"Then why," Millie said, her constant smile momentarily disappearing into puzzlement, "would Rath have gone along with it?"

"What do you mean?" I asked.

"Why would he have taken part in that stunt?"

I exchanged glances with the unusually silent Jill. She shrugged and smirked—you're on your own, brother.

So I said to the Arnolds, "Uh, who says he did?" I didn't know what else to say, short of expressing the view that the "stunt" hadn't been a stunt at all, but a real murder in which Rath (one would suppose) took only a reluctant part. Which I couldn't hope to prove without mentioning that I'd stumbled upon Rath's body in a condition consistent with the way he died in said "stunt."

"Oh, it was him, all right," Millie said.

Jill, interest piqued, cut in. "Why are you so sure?"

"Well," Carl said, ever deadpan, "I guess it's possible it was somebody else. Somebody playing Rath."

Millie said, "But Carl's right—Rath *was* around."

"What?" Jill and I said.

Carl said, "Rath only *pretended* to leave."

"Why do you say that?" I said, just me, though Jill no doubt was thinking it.

Millie lectured Carl, waggling a forefinger. "You don't *know* for a *fact* he pretended to leave. . . . He could've left and come back."

"Same difference," Carl shrugged.

"But who was he helping, by playing along?" Millie asked her husband. "Somebody on one of the teams?"

"What the hell are you two *talking* about?"

They looked at me, shocked to have heard such force coming from me, who after all was still wearing the Lester Denton facade. A little dab'll do ya.

"It's just that we saw him Thursday night," Millie said, shrugging elaborately, eyes wide, palms up.

"*After* he got mad and supposedly left," Carl added.

Jill asked, "When was this?"

"We were out walking in the snow," Millie said. "We were on that little gazebo bridge by the lake."

"What did you see?" I said, grasping Millie's arm.

She pulled back, wincing, not understanding my urgency. "Hey, take it easy! We didn't see anything, much—just Kirk Rath."

"Yeah," Carl said, thumbing through his notebook. "I jotted some notes. Wasn't sure it might not have something to do with the Mystery Weekend. We saw him out walking, along by the bushes near the lake, all by himself. It was about eleven fifteen. . . ."

But that was *after* I'd seen Rath killed!

I was mentally reeling, so it was Jill who asked, "Are you sure of this?"

"Sure," Carl deadpanned. "It seemed odd to me, that's all."

Now I had presence of mind to speak again: "What did?"

"The front of his jacket was all slashed, ripped up. But he was fine."

16

· · ·

That evening, at seven o'clock, the high-ceilinged pine dining hall transformed itself into a dimly lit night spot, where Frank Sinatra and big band music held sway. The snowstorm had prevented the arrival of the New York City-based dance band who'd been booked, but Mary Wright had put together a sound system and found a nice stack of smooth forties and fifties pop sides to create a nicely nostalgic aura; whether you were into Christie or Chandler, it didn't matter—all mystery fans like to slide into the past.

Mary Wright herself was playing d.j., in a pretty pink satin gown rather than a Mohonk blazer for a change, and I—looking pretty natty myself in my cream sports jacket and skinny blue tie and navy slacks—went up to her and asked if she had any Bobby Darin.

"I think I can round up 'Beyond the Sea,'" she said.

"Thanks. It's not a 'Queen of the Hop' crowd, anyway."

She smiled at that and it was a pretty, pretty nice smile; I wished things hadn't gotten tense between us. But what the hell, it kept Jill from pinching me.

I went back to our regular table, where a few of us—myself and Jill included—were finishing up dinner (as this was a dinner dance, after all). Sardini and I were having a Vienna nut torte (not the same one) and Jill was putting away some pumpkin pie. Jack Flint and his wife sat across from us, and Jack was having a drink. Quaker roots or not, the Mohonk dining room did serve drinks with the evening meal, if you insisted on it.

I hadn't. I wanted my brain nice and clear. While the day had been uneventful since my talks with Mary Wright and the Arnolds, I was still trying to make sense of what I'd learned. After the noon buffet, and before the afternoon panel on which Flint and Sardini and I discussed the recent comeback of the private-eye story, Jill and I had tried to put some of the pieces together—and hadn't gotten anywhere much.

Fact Number One: Kirk Rath had been seen by the Arnolds *after* I supposedly saw him killed.

How was that even possible? Were the Arnolds confused about the time, or maybe just confused in general? Or did they see somebody else who merely resembled Rath—but if so, how do you explain the shredded jacket?

Fact Number Two: Kirk Rath and Mary Wright and Curt's son Gary were college chums.

What did that mean? Nothing much that we could see, other than that Mary entered the circle of suspects by virtue of having previously known Rath.

Fact Number Three: Gary Culver (Culver being Curt Clark's real last name, as you may recall) had been homosexual.

Did *that* mean anything? If Kirk Rath was Gary's

college roommate, did that make *Rath* homosexual as well? And if so, so what?

The latter subject Jill and I had disagreed on hotly, in an afternoon brainstorming session in our room. I insisted that the notion that Rath might have been gay was nonsense. In college, as a rule, you're *assigned* roommates in dorms, particularly in the first year. So, the odds were (poor choice of words, admittedly) Gary and Kirk had become roommates by chance. Just because Gary had been gay, that hardly meant it figured Kirk was, too.

"Besides," I told her, "Rath was too conservative. Politically, he was a reactionary—he's taken stands on issues that make the Moral Majority look like the American Civil Liberties Union."

"A perfect reason to stay in the closet," Jill had said.

"He just wasn't the type."

"You mean, he wasn't particularly effeminate? Grow up, Mal. Don't expect every gay male to be a drag queen."

"Give me a break, will you? I've seen him at various mystery conventions and such, and he's always in the presence of a stunning girl."

"Girl or woman?"

"I'd call them 'girls'—late teens, early twenties."

"Have you ever seen him with the same girl twice?"

I thought about that.

"No," I said. "It's always been a different one, but then I've only seen him at three or four conventions."

"Real babes?" she asked, archly.

"Yeah—real babes."

"Prostitutes, perhaps?"

"Oh, Jill, don't be ridiculous—"

"A call girl makes a nice escort for a gay man who's pretending to be straight."

I gave her a take-my-word-for-it look. "Look, I've heard rumors that he was a real stud, okay?"

"Rumors fueled by his being seen with knockout women. I think Rath was trying a little too hard to seem heterosexual."

"Ah, I just don't buy it."

"Mal, he was a guy in his late twenties living in a houseful of men, right?"

"That's his place of business—they all work with him."

"I got a news flash for you, kiddo—at most businesses, you don't sleep in."

"I just don't buy it."

"Notice that you no longer can find any reasonable counter-arguments. Notice that you begin to sound like a broken record."

"Notice that you are getting obnoxious."

"Okay, okay," she said, patting the air. "Just think about it. . . . Rath was a guy who liked to smear people. He was politically conservative, a regular self-styled William F. Buckley of the mystery world. If—and I say only *if*—he were gay, wouldn't he be likely to hide it?"

"Jill—"

"If. Hypothetical time."

"If he were gay, yeah, I guess he might try to hide it."

"Somebody as hated as Rath, somebody as into smearing people as Rath, somebody who was very likely just as insecure as he was egotistical, sure as hell might have tried to keep his off-center sexual preference under wraps."

"I just can't buy it."

"Change the needle. When you called his business, which is to say his home, where he and all the boys bunked, where did they say he was going on vacation?"

"Well . . . after Mohonk, he was going into the city. New York."

"And didn't they say he couldn't be reached—that even his staff couldn't reach him.?"

"Yes. But I don't see . . ."

With elaborate theatricality, she said, "Why would the editor and publisher of the *Chronicler*, a magazine so intrinsically tied to the personal vision of selfsame editor and publisher, not tell even his own *staff* where he could be reached? Does that sound like reasonable business behavior to you?"

"Sometimes executives do like to get away, Jill. Sometimes they need to be able to get away from the pressure, and the phones. That's not so uncommon."

"Yeah, and maybe he went into New York from time to time, for a little taste of forbidden fruit."

"Bad, Jill. Very bad."

"A tacky remark, yes, but to the point, wouldn't you agree? A closeted homosexual—even if he is sharing that closet with a few other boys—might from time to time take a trip into the big city."

"I suppose."

"I rest my case."

I gave the movie buff a slice of the world's worst W.C. Fields impression: "And a pretty case it is on which you're resting, my dear," adding, natural voice, "although your argument is considerably less attractive. And even if you were right—even if Rath were a homosexual—what would that have to do with his murder?"

"I don't know. But it does open up a range of motives that have nothing to do with literary criticism, doesn't it?"

Yes it did. And it had been eating at me, a hungry mouse nibbling at the cheese between my ears.

Tim Culver had come over to the table to stand and

talk to the seated Jack Flint; Pete Christian, who'd been sitting next to Tom, had gotten up, due to his usual restlessness, and wandered over into the conversation. Pete was congratulating Culver on the movie sale. Then one of the Mystery Weekenders approached Pete with a copy of his *Films of Charlie Chan* in one hand, and Jack's *Black Mask* doubled with Culver's *McClain's Score* in the other. There had been an autograph session this afternoon at tea time in the Lake Lounge, with all the authors present; it had been just after the panel Jack and Tom and I'd been on. But a few of the Weekenders had not made it to the session, possibly because they were sequestered with their respective teams, working on the latest batch of clues and info pertaining to *The Case of the Curious Critic*, as gathered during the final interrogation session late this morning.

While Jack, Tim, and Pete stood signing books, Cynthia Crystal, a martini in hand, silver skin of a gown covering her, glided over and asked us when we were going to stop eating and start dancing. I had put the torte well away, by this point, but Jill was taking her time with the pumpkin pie.

So, with Jill's blessing, I escorted Cynthia out onto the dance floor, where Bobby Darin was singing "The Good Life," and held her as close as I could and not get us killed by Culver and/or Jill.

"I shouldn't have been so cruel," she said, "that time you threw that pass."

She was referring to that Bouchercon where, several years ago, we'd met; she and I'd hung around a good deal together there, and I mistook it for romance when it was apparently just friendship.

"I shouldn't have thrown it," I said, still embarrassed. "I was out of line."

"Maybe," she said, a smile crinkling one corner of

her thin, pretty mouth. "And maybe it was a missed opportunity on my part."

"You're going to be a happily married woman soon."

"I'll be married," she said, seeking a wistful tone. "But how happy I'll be with a dour lug like Tim is debatable."

"Why marry him, then?"

"I love him."

"Yeah," I said, shaking my head. "That's usually how I get in jams, too."

She laughed a little, and it seemed less brittle than usual.

"Does anybody ever call you Cindy?" I asked her.

"Just my Aunt Cynthia."

"You just aren't the Cindy type, are you?"

"Sometimes I wish I were."

I laughed, and held her a little closer. "No you don't. You're exactly who you want to be."

She pulled away, appraising me, her smile cunning. "And who is that?"

"The smartest, prettiest, bitchiest gal around; the queen of the mystery writers."

She sighed, pleasantly. "That sounds vaguely sexist."

"What, 'bitchiest' or 'gal'?"

"No—'queen.' "

"Ellery didn't mind," I reminded her.

She pretended to be irritated. "Did you bring me out here to flirt with me or tease me or what?"

"I brought you out here to dance."

"I doubt that. You always have an ulterior motive. And we were at a dance together, at that Bouchercon, once upon a time. You sat out the whole bloody thing."

"I only dance when they play Bobby Darin records."

She rolled her eyes. "Spare me that Darin rap—I know all about your eccentric tastes."

"Such as you being my favorite female mystery writer?"

She pursed her lips in a nasty smile. "You're being sexist again."

"Did I say 'female'?"

"You most certainly did."

"I meant to say 'lady'."

"Oh, that's so much better."

Darin was replaced on the turntable by that upstart Sinatra—"Strangers in the Night," of all things. You wouldn't catch Bobby singing scoobie doobie doo.

We kept dancing anyway. I sprung my ulterior-motive question: "What's the deal with Tim and Pete Christian?"

"Pardon?"

"He and Pete seem to be getting along great."

And they did: they were both sitting at our table now, chatting, although Pete was doing most of the talking.

"Why shouldn't they be?" she asked.

"Well, Pete's very bitter about what Rath did to his friend C.J. Beaufort; blames him for his death. And it was Tim's interview in the *Chronicler* that supposedly put Beaufort over the edge. . . ."

"Oh that," she said, dismissively. "Tim smoothed that over with Pete right after Beaufort's suicide."

"How?"

She shrugged; it made her blonde hair shimmer in the dim lighting. "Tim's known Pete for years," she said. "He was well aware that Beaufort was Pete's mentor. So he immediately called Pete and expressed his sympathy and said he'd never forgive himself for that interview. That 'goddamn interview,' to be exact."

"And Pete understood?"

"Sure. Pete was burned by an interview in the *Chronicler*, too."

"How so?"

"Same sort of thing as Tim—he was encouraged to be freewheeling in front of a tape recorder, and at the same time was promised that he'd get to edit the transcript before publication. Dear little Kirk didn't send Pete the transcript, of course, and the published version embarrassed Pete royally—or so he says. I read the interview and didn't see anything Pete needed to be sorry for having said."

"Still," I said, "that's infuriating, being betrayed like that."

"I hear the *Chronicler's* cleaned up its act," she said, "in that regard at least. It got to the point where nobody in the business would grant them an interview till they started offering their various interviewees certain assurances in writing."

After Sinatra scoobied his last doobie, we walked over to the table, and Cynthia moved on, and I sat next to Jill. She was a vision in a black-and-white sequined square-shouldered gown. A smirking vision.

"You two were pretty cozy," she said.

"Old friends."

"As opposed to strangers in the night."

"Let's dance," I said.

"It isn't a Bobby Darin song."

It was Sinatra again, from a better period: "Summer Wind."

"I'll make an exception," I said.

We danced, and I asked her why she seemed so jealous this weekend; it really wasn't like her.

"I told you why," she said.

"You mean because we're going to be going our separate ways before long."

She bit her lip and nodded.

"We don't have to," I said.

"I know. But it would mean we'd have to compromise—or at least one of us would."

"You mean, you'd have to agree to stay in Port City, or I'd have to agree to pull up stakes and head out on the prairie with you, rounding up cable rustlers or whatever it is you do."

"You know exactly what it is I do."

"Yeah, and you're good at it."

"I'm—I'm not so good at compromise, though."

"Compromise isn't something either of us does too well," I said.

"I know."

Sinatra sang.

"It's a few months away," I said. "Let's not talk about it."

"I love you, Nick."

"I love you, Nora."

We held each other and danced and Sinatra sang. He wasn't Bobby Darin, but we made do.

17

• • •

We mingled the rest of the evening with our fellow suspects in the *Curious Critic* case, and with the various Mystery Weekenders, most of whom seemed a little keyed up, what with the big presentations coming the very next morning. But Jill and I refrained from doing any detecting, which is to say carrying on any conversations with hidden purposes.

With one exception.

Curt had been keeping his wife Kim out on the dance floor most of the evening; he seemed almost to be wooing her. But there was something wrong—Curt was trying awfully hard, doing all the talking; Kim seemed distracted, even a little morose.

But she looked wonderful—superficially anyway. She was poured into another gown, not unlike the black one she'd worn in her role as Roark Sloth's ex-wife in the weekend mystery, only this one was white. She looked as pretty as ever, in that exaggerated cartoony way of hers, and sexy as ever, too, her breasts doing a first-rate Jayne Mansfield impression.

Only her eyes gave her away, her big brown eyes. They were dull and red and baggy.

Curt finally left her alone, at their table, some Mystery Weekenders dragging him away for autographs. I noted this from the dance floor, and Jill and I made a bee-line for her. We sat on her either side.

"You look terrific tonight," Jill said. "You're going to be a big movie star someday and I'm going to brag about knowing you."

"Thanks," Kim said, dully.

This seemed short of what I'd expect from bubbly Kim, who, like any actress, had an ego at least as large as, well, Jayne Manfield's.

"You're stunning in that gown," I said, trying to coax some conversation. "But I thought you didn't like tight clothes?"

"Curt likes me in them," she said, distractedly.

"Kim, are you okay? What's wrong?"

She smiled bravely. "Nothing."

"Could I steal you for a dance? Curt's tied up."

"No—no, I don't think so." There was a drink before her, Scotch on the melting rocks; she sipped it, hungrily.

"How did the interrogation go this morning?" I asked her.

She looked at me sharply. "What?"

"Uh, when you played your part."

"My . . . part?"

"When you played Sloth's ex-wife."

"Oh. That. That went fine."

She sipped some more Scotch.

I took aim. "Curt told you, didn't he?"

She looked at me with narrowed eyes. Said nothing.

"He told you about Rath."

She looked into the drink.

"He told you about what Jill and I found on our mountain hike yesterday."

She sucked air quickly in, let it slowly out. Then she said, "Yes."

I had thought as much, from the look of her.

I put my hand on her bare arm, which felt cold. "I'm sorry you're going through this," I said. "It's a burden knowing, trying to keep up a party facade."

She nodded.

"It'll be okay," I said, squeezing her arm a little, in what I hoped was a reassuring manner. "The snow's stopped. The plows will be out soon. The police will be here before long."

"I wish he hadn't told me," she said.

I shrugged. "Husbands tell wives things. It's hard to keep a secret like that from somebody you're living with."

She smiled tightly, meaninglessly, stood, said, "Would you excuse me?"

"Sure," I said, and she was up and gone.

"She's been crying," Jill said.

"Murder could spoil anybody's weekend," I said. "I'm all danced out. How about you?"

"Yeah," she said. "Isn't there a movie pretty soon?"

I groaned. "Don't tell me we're going to do tonight's movie?"

"It's Mickey Spillane as Mike Hammer in *The Girl Hunters*."

"Fitting of Pete to select that," I admitted, interested in spite of myself. "An author playing a role in a mystery. Well, I can't resist the Mick as Mike. You talked me into it."

"I want to freshen up," she said, standing. "Coming?"

I checked my watch; ten till eleven. The movie was at eleven-thirty.

"I haven't had a chance to talk to Janis Flint yet," I said. "Let me do that, and I'll join you at the room."

She said fine, and left, and I searched out the Flints; they were standing by an open support beam, talking with the Arnolds and the Logans—rival team players ganging up on a couple of suspects. On cue, "Beyond the Sea" hit the turntable, and I asked Mrs. Flint for the dance. She smiled and accepted.

She looked quietly lovely in a floor-length floral gown, albeit vegetarian thin; she was a wisp of a thing in my arms, and we floated around to the Darin strains. She had on a little more makeup than usual, and I was quite taken with her eyes, a soft green with flecks of black. Jack Flint was a lucky man.

"How did your interrogation sessions go?" I asked.

"Very nicely," she said. "Your encouragement was just the boost I needed."

"What role were you playing exactly?"

"Sloth's older sister Emma," she said. "The last person known to have seen him alive."

"Did you kill him?"

She smiled in an unaffected way that Cynthia Crystal had only heard about. "I'll never tell," she said.

I laughed, and we floated some more.

As I walked her slowly over toward her husband, I asked, "How bitter is Jack about Kirk Rath's bad reviews? I heard him say the *Chronicler's* keeping him out of the book market."

"That's just Jack talking," she said with a quick dismissive shrug. "Both Mysterious Press and Walker are after him for another book. The editors are eager to get him back."

"So why doesn't he go back to it?"

"He will. He's just amassing some 'Hollywood money,' as he calls it. When he's built us some security, he'll be back to writing his novels. Wait and see."

"I'm relieved to hear that. So, then ... how would you rate his bitterness toward Rath?"

"On a scale of one to ten? Seven."

"Okay," I said, smiling a little, and handing her over to her husband, with whom I stood and chatted briefly, before heading back to the room.

The halls were deserted, of course, everybody back partying at the dance, and I again thought of *The Shining* and wondered if that kid on his Big Wheel would finally come rounding the next corner to run me down. My feet padded on the carpet and I watched them walk, as my mind sorted through tidbits I'd picked up tonight.

So Jack Flint's bitterness toward Rath was a seven on a scale of one to ten. That hardly seemed a murder motive; particularly when you considered that Jack Flint was making a small fortune in TV and movie writing.

And Curt had told his wife about Rath's murder. That didn't surprise me much—as I'd said to Kim, most husbands in his situation *would* have shared that awful secret. It's not the kind of thing you can keep to yourself; if you swallowed it, it'd just burn a hole in your stomach.

As for Pete Christian and Tim Culver, there seemed to be no enmity there, despite Tim's inadvertent role in C. J. Beaufort's suicide. That didn't make either of them less a suspect though, did it? If anything, it opened up a new possibility: a team effort to wipe out Rath.

I'd also learned that the only person who called Cynthia Crystal "Cindy" was her Aunt Cynthia. The question was, where was Cynthia's aunt when Rath was killed?

Screw it, I thought, and a hand settled on my shoulder and jerked me around.

A red-faced Rick Fahy was standing there; he was in

evening clothes—I'd spotted him at the dance, earlier—and apparently he'd followed me.

"What do you want?" I said irritably, picking his hand off my shoulder like a scab.

"This," he said and smacked me.

I took it on the side of the jaw, and it didn't feel good, swinging my face to one side, but one thing about my jaw is, it ain't glass, nor am I slow to react, and I threw one back at him.

And he deflected it with a karate-style swipe of a hand; I sensed I was in deep shit. Where was Carl Arnold when you needed him?

Fahy grabbed me by the lapels of my sports coat and flung me against the nearest wall; I slid down and just sat. It was humbling being tossed around by somebody smaller than me.

Nonetheless, I got up and charged him, and he stepped aside and sent me crashing into another wall, like an outfoxed bull. But I braced with my hands, didn't hit my head, and managed to turn and give him a sharp elbow in his side.

That hurt him, and he stumbled back, and I sent a good right hand into his face and bloodied his nose some.

He did not go down, though, tough little bastard; and when I threw my left, he deflected it again, karate style, speaking of which, his next blow was a sideways chop to my stomach, which doubled me over, and all the wind in me went south as first my knees, then my head, hit the floor.

He climbed on the back of me, like I was a bronc, forcing me flat on my stomach. I wondered, idly, why we were fighting. Only we weren't fighting anymore, were we? I had lost.

He grabbed a fistful of my hair and yanked back, till

I thought my Adam's apple would punch through my throat.

"You're going to tell me what you know," he said.

Then he let go of my hair and my head flopped forward and hit the carpeted floor. Ouch.

I said, "Any particular subject?" It was hard to get it out; my wind was barely back.

"Kirk Rath," he said.

"He's dead."

There was silence.

I felt him climb off my back. I rolled on my side. Fahy was stumbling; it was like I'd gotten in that telling lick that when we were fighting I never managed to. He braced himself against the wall, like a drunk.

I got on my feet somehow.

"Are you okay?" I asked him. I shouldn't have cared, but I could tell already he was in worse shape than me.

He swallowed, thickly. "Tell me what you know," he said. It wasn't a demand, this time. In fact, he added, rather pathetically I thought, "Please."

So I told him. I stood next to him in the hall while he leaned against the wall and I told him everything, from what I'd seen outside my window, to finding the body, to such strange items as the Arnolds claiming to have seen Rath *after* he'd seemed to have been killed.

About halfway through, he began crying.

Quietly. Tears just rolling down a face that seemed impassive if you didn't notice the quivering.

A while after that he sat on the floor. Crying. Still crying. Listening to my story. By this time I was sitting next to him.

"You were his lover, weren't you?" I asked.

Fahy nodded.

"Did he tell you he was going to storm out Thursday night like he did?"

"N-no. I was as surprised as anybody. He told me

we'd be seeing plenty of each other this weekend." He sighed, raggedly. "Carefully, of course."

I chewed on that for a minute.

Then I said, "Remember that little lounge area, where I played Lester Denton?"

He looked at me, narrowed his eyes, shook his head yes.

"Meet me there at eleven-thirty."

"W-why?"

"I'm going to round some people up," I said. "We may be able to sort this thing out before the police get here."

He nodded again; I helped him up. Me, the guy he'd just beat the everliving crap out of, helping him up. The poor bastard.

I knocked on the door of our room and Jill answered it, her eyes going very round and very wide.

"What the hell happened to you?"

"I think I just figured out who killed Kirk Rath," I said, licking some blood out of the corner of my mouth. "Though I hope to hell I'm wrong."

18

• • •

It was nearly midnight by the time everybody showed up. There was some grumbling, but everybody made it: I'd enlisted Tom and Jill, and we tracked everybody down just as the dance was starting to dwindle. Pete, who'd had to impose on a friend to change reels for him on the film currently showing in the Parlor, was the last to arrive; he'd somehow found time to change into a sweater. The rest, still in their evening clothes, mostly sat on the plush furniture, some of them squirming, others just going with the flow, chatting, basking in the soft yellow light; the shadows of the flames from the fireplace flickering over them. The exceptions were Mary Wright, who leaned against a pillar in the background, brooding, and Cynthia Crystal, who sat on a bench at the nearby baby grand, noodling various Cole Porter tunes. Tim Culver, a drink in hand, stood nearby, leaning against the piano.

We'd have the small sitting room to ourselves—the

Mystery Weekenders were either at Pete's movie in the Parlor or holed up in their rooms preparing their presentations. An occasional gamester might wander by, but this party would be a private one. No one would even think to crash it.

Two of my invited guests were roaming, a bit. Pete Christian, chainsmoking, was pacing as usual, sitting only occasionally; and Curt Clark stood by the fireplace, encouraging the fire with an iron poker, at one point tossing a log on. His wife Kim sat nearby in a big thronelike chair with her hands folded in her lap, looking in her tight low-cut gown like an overdeveloped and emotionally battered teenage girl.

The only one irritated, however, was Jack Flint, leaning forward in his seat like an angry bear, his wife putting a slight but restraining hand on his arm. "What's this about?" he growled. "I wanted to see that movie. I never got a chance to see it before."

"I'll send you a video cassette," I told him flatly, giving him a look that said I wasn't kidding around here. That seemed to momentarily calm him. I was standing; I'd prepared the seating before the others arrived to create a sort of semicircle—although Cynthia had chosen to sit outside of it, at the piano—with me near the fireplace. Curt was now sitting, on the arm of Kim's chair, near the fireplace, which he continued to now and then prod with the wrought-iron poker, reaching in his long-limbed way from where he sat.

Curt and Kim were at my left; Jill was sitting at my right, and next to her was a putty-faced Rick Fahy—the life seemed drained out of him. The warmth of the fireplace was to my back.

"I asked you all here," I said, "so that we might be able to prepare ourselves for the police, who should be arriving within the hour."

"The *police*?" Flint said, and his stunned look was a

typical reaction; questions came from everybody all at once, words tumbling on top of each other, but I made a stop motion with my hands, pushing back the air.

"This will take a while," I said, "but I intend to explain everything that I know—and then to share some speculations with you. Frankly, I intend to share these speculations in the hope that I'm wrong. I want to confront the person I suspect before I share any suspicions with the police; and I want to share those suspicions with all of you, in case some of you might have something pertinent to add. And, to be quite honest with you, I would like to put everything I know, and everything I suspect, out in the open *now*—before the police arrive—in the hopes that we might arrive at some conclusion among ourselves . . . since, like you, I will soon be a suspect in a murder investigation."

The place went up for grabs, of course, but I quieted them down, by gesturing and waving as if they were a rebellious choral group I was directing.

"Please don't ask any questions," I said, forcing my voice above their collective one. "I think I can anticipate most of your questions, and after I've put the basic facts before you, you can grill me all you want."

Curt Clark said, "Let Mal speak. He's been wanting to report a murder all weekend."

"Thank you, Curt," I said. "And he's right. All of you know about the 'prank' I witnessed outside my window Thursday night. What only a few of you know—specifically, Curt, Kim, Mary Wright, Jill Forrest and I—is that Kirk Rath really *was* murdered."

They kept it down this time, but they were whispering among themselves, heads were shaking, *Is that guy crazy or what?*, but all eyes were on yours truly. I had the floor; I hadn't had so much attention since I played Lester Denton this morning in this same little parlor.

I told them about the mountain hike and how Jill and

I had found Rath's body; also that the police chief had asked the few of us who knew about the murder to keep mum for the time being—a directive I now felt compelled to ignore.

"So the prank wasn't a prank," Tom Sardini said, matter-of-factly. He wasn't a guy who fazed easily. "Rath was killed outside your window, and somebody hauled his body in Rath's own car up to Sky Top and dumped it."

"That's how it looks," I said. "But why do that? The body was bound to be found there before very long; if it hadn't started snowing yesterday, there'd have been other hikers out besides Jill and me, and the body would've been found even sooner. That's a standard hike to take when you're visiting Mohonk."

Jack Flint, his irritation gone, was somber as he said, "You don't hide a body out in the open like that—not with all these woods around."

"Exactly my point," I said. "Somebody wanted that body found while we were all still here."

"Why?" Flint asked.

"To get the inevitable investigation over with," I said. "We were all invited here because we had real-life motives to kill Kirk Rath. Oh, some of us aren't really very convincing suspects, I'll grant you. As I pointed out to somebody earlier tonight, you generally don't kill somebody over a bad review. But Kirk Rath was no ordinary reviewer. He caused a lot of misery—Pete blames him for a death and so does Tim Culver. Most of us have suffered career setbacks because of Rath. Face it. . . . We're suspects. That's why we were invited here."

Curt stood and said, "But *I* invited you here, Mal. I invited all of you here."

"I know. But then, unless I'm very mistaken—and God knows I hope I am, Curt—you killed Kirk Rath."

Curt's smile was faint; the shadows of flames from

the nearby fireplace reflected off his glasses and made him look just a little crazy. Which is exactly what he was.

But he was also smart and shrewd, and he said, "Don't be silly. I couldn't have killed Rath. You and I spoke on the telephone, just moments before you saw him killed." He pointed at me like Humphrey Bogart pointing at Mary Astor. "And you yourself said the killer was a stocky man; in case you haven't noticed, I'm about six-three in my bare feet."

"For the record, I didn't say Rath's supposed assailant was a man; I said 'person.' It could've been a woman."

Cynthia had long since stopped noodling at the piano; she was quite serious as she asked, "Why do you say 'supposed assailant'? Haven't you been saying all along that what you saw outside your window was a real killing?"

I laughed a little. "I sure have. Because Curt was right, from the very beginning—what I saw *was* a prank. A 'Grand Guignol farce,' as he put it, staged for my benefit."

Now people were shaking their heads and shifting in their seats and climbing all over each's attempt to tell me how ridiculous I was.

"Wait," I said, holding up my hand, palm out, stop. "Just wait."

They quieted, somewhat reluctantly.

I said, "Curt wrote, produced, and directed that skit; but he didn't appear in it. He had an accomplice for that. But consider this—he and Mary Wright have been making all the arrangements for the weekend—"

From the back of the room, Mary Wright said, "I had nothing to do with this—leave me out of this!"

I ignored her, pressed on: "The point is, Curt knew well in advance which room was mine. In fact, Thursday evening, he dropped by and looked it over ... walked to the window and glanced out, like a producer checking out the theater the afternoon before the night the curtain goes up on his new show. Oh, and he was ready for that curtain to go up. Before I checked in, he'd been in that room—for one thing, he dragged my phone from the nightstand over to a table by the window. Having the phone by the window allowed him to call me later, supposedly about a scheduling crisis caused by Rath's leaving, but in reality merely making sure I was right there at the window to witness the show he was staging. He even directed my attention where it was supposed to be, by asking me to look out my window to see if it was snowing yet. Also, he'd jammed my window shut, beforehand—superglue, nails, what have you. Somehow he made sure that window wouldn't open, to keep me from getting into the act."

Curt said, "I wish you'd refrain from referring to me in the third person. And, if I might add, this is the most harebrained plot you've ever come up with. Just who was playing the role of Kirk Rath in this supposed charade of mine?"

"It was typecasting," I said. "Rath was playing himself."

I expected a chorus of *what's* from my audience, but they had settled down, now. They had decided I was worth listening to. I hadn't convinced anybody yet, but they were willing to listen.

"When I found Rath's body on those rocks, two things struck me—first, his face was passive, not contorted, as it had been when I'd seen him slashed outside my window. This, on reflection, suggests to me that Rath's face might have been slashed after he was dead, as part of an effort to keep his corpse consistent with what I'd witnessed. Second, when I checked his pockets I found his envelope of instructions, like the one I'd been sent by Curt for my role in the mystery weekend. But if you'll recall, we all received two things: a list of our fellow suspects in Roark Sloth's murder; and, for our eyes only, a description of our own role in the weekend's festivities. In Rath's envelope, however, I found only the list of suspects. Not the instructions for his *own* part. Why? I think it's because the murderer— which is to say, you, Curt—destroyed that sheet."

Pretending amusement, Curt said, "And why should I do that?"

"Because it would reveal that Kirk Rath was only playing the game you outlined for him to play."

He laughed at that, glancing at Kim, shaking his head; she wasn't laughing.

"You instructed Kirk Rath to throw that tantrum and leave," I said to him. "You told him that that was part of his role this weekend—to storm out, pretend to leave . . . but then appear near my window later and, with someone's help, play-act a murder."

"That's preposterous."

"The Mohonk Mystery Weekend thrives on the pre-posterous. The scenario I've just suggested is very much in keeping with the activities here. My guess is that Rath thought he was supposed to make a surprise reappearance the next morning, perhaps after the sus-pect interrogation; he probably planned to sneak back in, to a room you arranged, later Thursday night, possi-bly wearing a ski mask to keep from being recog-nized—or he could have stayed in a motel in New Paltz. That detail I'm not sure of. But I feel very sure that Rath—like so many of the game-players here this weekend—thought the prank was a part of the mystery. Hell, the Arnolds and the Logans have as much as hit me over the head with that . . . that it *had* to be part of the Mystery Weekend, in which case it could only be the work of one person: Curt Clark."

Curt's smile seemed nervous now; twitching, just a little. "How," he asked, rather archly, "did all of this lead Kirk Rath to Sky Top and his grisly fate?"

"You asked him to meet you there. He was like the rest of us—he'd received his instructions by mail and needed some on-the-spot final instruction, final coaching. You told him to drive up to Sky Top after the 'stunt,' where you could speak privately, without giving away the joke you and he'd pulled on the Mystery Weekenders. And, in return for his cooperation, you killed him."

Curt was smiling, shaking his head.

"He trusted you—you'd been friends for years. Some friend. You slashed him, you stabbed him; it was very brutal. You hated him. Enough to kill him that savage way, enough to plot it like one of your mystery stories—intricately, cleverly."

He ignored that, saying, "How did you come up with this theory? You have no proof whatsoever; it's the purest of speculation, based on almost nothing."

"Not really. One of the couples here—the Arnolds, I mentioned them before—said they saw Kirk Rath skulking around out in the snow, *after* what I'd seen out my window. That's what got me thinking about the possibility of the so-called prank being a for-real prank."

He wasn't smiling now; his expression was blank, though he held his head back, rather patricianly, I thought.

"Also," I said, gesturing over to the expressionless Fahy, "this gentleman was a good friend of Rath's. His name is Rick Fahy, as some of you know, and he writes for *The Mystery Chronicler*. He is here at Mohonk as a game-player, as a matter of fact—to write about the Mystery Weekend from the perspective of a participant. Kirk Rath told Mr. Fahy, here, that they'd be spending a good deal of time together this weekend. I take this to mean Rath intended to stay around."

"That doesn't mean he didn't storm out on impulse," Tim Culver said. He was still standing over by Cynthia, but he was challenging me with hard eyes that crossed the distance easily. I was putting his brother on trial, after all.

I said, "Mr. Fahy insists that he would have at least had a phone call from Rath, in the aftermath of that; and he didn't."

Pete, who was smoking and pacing along the right wall, stopped to ask: "Why didn't Rath tell his friend Fahy about the prank, if that's what it was? That he'd be pretending to leave and all?"

"Rath and Mr. Fahy were very close," I said. "So close that I believe Rath *would* have told his friend all about it—under any circumstances but one: Rath had assigned Mr. Fahy to a story for the *Chronicler*—and the dictates of that story were that Mr. Fahy play the game like everybody else. Rath would've been breaking the rules—and spoiling the story for his magazine—if he shared his role-playing secrets with Mr. Fahy."

"It wasn't even my idea to invite Kirk Rath," Curt said, openly defensive now.

"No," I admitted. "It was Mary Wright's. And she told me she had great difficulty talking you into coming to Mohonk to stage the mystery.... That is, until she mentioned her idea about inviting Kirk Rath. And that's when you said yes to Mary Wright. Because that's when your mystery-writer mind started whirring. *Only* a mystery writer could commit a murder like this. Only Curt Clark could commit a murder so convoluted, so nasty, so ... cute."

"I'd take that as a compliment," Curt said, "had I really done all this."

"Then convince me that you didn't," I said, meaning

it. "I don't want you to be guilty. You're my friend. You gave me my first career break. I learned half of what I know about writing from you. I look up to you. Goddammit, Curt—tell me I'm wrong. Convince me I'm wrong."

Curt studied me and something human flickered in his eyes, behind the glass, or maybe it was just the shadows of the flames.

But all he could find to say was, "It's your show. Try to make it play. See if you can."

"Damn you, anyway. You know me too well. You knew how I'd react. That I'd buy what I saw out that window as real, and then you were right there, weren't you, telling me it was a prank. But you knew me better than that—you knew I'd ask around. That I'd have to look into this."

"Why would any 'murderer' invite that?"

"It was partly arrogance. But it was mostly a very clever way of clouding what really happened. You made me your alibi . . . and *what* an alibi! Through me, you'd sell the cops that the murder had been committed Thursday night, outside my window. From my description of the killer, and because we'd just been talking on the phone, you'd be clear. No one would be asking questions about what you were doing an hour *after* I saw the 'murder'—when you were *really* killing Rath, up on the mountain, your goddamn knife flashing in the moonlight."

"How writerly," Curt said.

"Shut up," I said. "You did it. You even sucked your poor wife in."

Kim was covering her face with her hand; she was weeping, probably. The room was dim enough, you couldn't tell.

"She was in my room," Curt said. "You heard me

talking to her, when you came to our room, moments after what you saw—"

"I heard *you* talk to her," I said. "I didn't hear her reply, and I certainly didn't see her. No, she was your accomplice—unwitting in my opinion. Like Rath, she thought the prank was a part of the Mystery Weekend. She's an actress, and a good one. She has the know-how to do the makeup, to stage the stunt; bundled up, in a ski mask, she made a convincing 'killer,' But she wasn't in on it, not the real murder. I saw how shattered she was today, having found out Rath was really dead. You told her about it now, so you could manipulate her public behavior later. What, did you assure her you *didn't* do it, but that if anybody ever found out about the 'murder' prank you'd both been involved in with Rath, no one would understand, and you could both be innocently dragged down? Something like that. Anyway, Kim doesn't have it in her to have gone along with your loony plan. She may stand behind you—cover for you. She may do that. There isn't much she wouldn't do for you—from dressing to please you, to putting her career on hold so she could try to give you a second family, a second chance, which you should've taken. She loves you. Love makes people do deranged things. Like it made you do."

"Love?" Curt said.

"Love for you son. He died six months ago, just twenty-six, of pneumonia. That struck me as strange, when Kim mentioned it. She said something else that threw me, though I didn't think much about it at the time—that you were moving out of Greenwich Village because it was getting too 'lavender' for your tastes, Curt. That hit me funny, because for one thing, Greenwich Village didn't just suddenly go lavender; even somebody from Iowa knows gays have been a part of the Village scene since around the dawn of time. But I also didn't take you for somebody who'd be bigoted to-ward gays; I never saw it in you before, and in fact you've always been liberal in every way, the epitome of the hip New Yorker."

Curt was standing looking into the fire, now.

"Then Mary Wright told me how she'd dated Gary for a while, in college, but they couldn't make a go of it. Seems that first year, Gary had come to a realization: he was gay."

Just looking into the fire.

"You worshipped your son, your only son, the only one of your first marriage; you loved your wife, your first wife, Joan, very much—and Gary was all you had left of her. You carry one of his paintings around with you, wherever you go. You love him, even now, to the point of obsession. But he was gay. Why, when your be-loved son had been gay, did you suddenly begin to *hate* gays?"

He turned to look at me sharply, and almost an-swered; but then he looked back at the fire, as if the flames were hypnotizing him.

"Why," I asked, "would a twenty-six-year-old man die of pneumonia? It's hard to say; hard even to hazard a guess, why that would happen in this day and age. But add something to the description—a *gay* twenty-six-year-old man—and another possibility arises: Ac-quired Immune Deficiency Syndrome. AIDS—a disease you don't die from, not exactly. . . . It just destroys your body's immune systems. So that a healthy young man is suddenly dead of pneumonia."

Cynthia Crystal had come over to put her arm around Kim, who was weeping openly now, into a handker-chief.

"I'm only guessing," I said, "but I think, Curt, you blamed your son's gay life-style for his death. That's *your* oversimplification, not mine, of course—AIDS is hardly God's punishment for homosexuality, but it did allow you to focus *blame* somewhere. Suddenly sophisticated Curt Clark finds Greenwich Village 'too lavender.' But blaming gays in general for Gary's death wasn't enough. You had to get specific."

Curt turned to look at me; he was leaning against the hearth—he was sweating, he was so close to the flames. His expression was tortured. He said, "And how did I do that?"

"You blamed the person who introduced your son to the gay life-style: his college roommate, Kirk Rath."

Some gasps came from my little audience; Rath's homosexuality had indeed been well closeted.

I went on, relentlessly; "You convinced yourself that if it hadn't been for the unhappy circumstances of Gary drawing a gay roommate who, in your mind anyway, seduced him into that world, he might have led a happy, healthy, straight life. Why, he'd be alive today."

Curt swallowed. He said, "Wouldn't he?" Bitterness tinged his words, but it was a question; some doubt was there.

"Who can say? But you didn't have any right to blame Rath; you can't know for sure what was in your son's heart, his mind. You don't really know that Rath was, in fact, your son's first brush with homosexuality. Logic and experience would say, probably not. It's too easy an answer to blame a 'seducer' like Rath for the road your son chose to go down. Rath was a pretty rotten guy, but he didn't deserve that rap; but perhaps his mean-spiritedness makes a little more sense, now that we know that he lived a public lie, a smug facade behind which an unhappy man with a secret hid. If his public political and moral stance is to be at all believed, it's a secret he was no doubt ashamed of. Did he give you all those good reviews because he knew you knew about his past, knew the truth about him? No matter. It is a little ironic, of course, that he invoked the wrath of a mystery writer like you ... like me, like all of us poor schmucks in this business who write about a world where mysteries can be solved and blame can be placed and wrongs can be righted. The real world just isn't like that. And when you treat the real world like it's a mystery story, Curt—you're going to make a mess of things. A real mess."

Curt smiled; turned to me. He was still near the fire, but he wasn't leaning against the hearth anymore. He had his composure back, one hundred percent. But his eyes behind the dark-rimmed glasses were still tortured.

He said, "If you expect me to confirm or deny any of what you've said, I'm afraid you're in for a disappointment. I applaud your audacious, if convoluted, plotting, but I would suggest that I'm only one of a roomful of suspects, here ... and neither you, nor the police, will ever manage to single me successfully out from the pack."

Then Curt took a sudden step backward, looking past me, startled, and suddenly I was pushed to one side, something, somebody moving past me like a goddamn freight train. The audience I'd assembled was on its feet, now, calling out, crying out, as they and I saw Rick Fahy grab the iron poker and lift it and with one swift stroke, one savage blow, cave in the side of Curt Clark's head.

Fahy got in another bash before I pulled him back, by both elbows, and he struggled for a moment, but then relaxed, and dropped the bloody poker with a clunk, as he ... as I ... as we ... saw Curt slump to the floor. His brains were showing. Those clever, creative brains; exposed. He flopped forward, and Kim began screaming.

Jack Flint took charge of Fahy, pasty-faced, slack-jawed, limp, just some flesh and bones flung into evening clothes; and Cynthia and Culver were restraining

Kim, whose screaming was subsiding into sobs, while I leaned over Curt's body and touched the side of his face. His glasses had come off. His eyes were open, wide. But they didn't seem tortured now. That was something, anyway.

"Shit, Curt—damn it all, anyway. I'm sorry—I'm sorry. . . ." He couldn't hear me, I suppose; but I had to say it. I was as responsible for this as Fahy, in a way; but not as responsible as Curt Clark.

Jill was at my side, pulling me up, helping me, making me stand. "Mal, I'm sorry—so very sorry."

"It wasn't supposed to happen this way," I said.

"Nothing happens the way it's supposed to," she said. Neither one of us felt much like Nick or Nora.

PART FOUR
...
Sunday

19

· · ·

At ten o'clock the next morning—the time that had been set aside for the solutions to Curt Clark's *Case of the Curious Critic*—a haggard Mary Wright in an uncharacteristically wrinkled blue Mohonk blazer stood before the three hundred or so assembled Mystery Weekenders in the Parlor and gave a brief, apologetic explanation about why this morning's festivities had been cancelled.

"A tragic series of events has eclipsed our make-believe mystery," she said into the microphone, her amplified voice sounding hollow. "The mystery community has lost two of its most interesting, respected figures: in separate, but related, turns of extreme, unfortunate circumstance, both Kirk Rath and Curt Clark have lost their lives. Out of respect to their memories, our mystery this weekend must go unsolved. If we might have a few moments of silence . . ."

The old cough-drop boys in the high framed pictures looked down in their Quaker way on us poor sinners as we each in his or her own fashion said good-bye to two tragically linked men.

Then Mary put on a small, intrepid smile and said, "For those of you interested, we are providing a raincheck of sorts to any of you wishing to attend either of next year's Mystery Weekends. Also, a partial refund will be sent to each and every one of you, as we were not able to deliver our entire package as promised."

Business considerations. Death was the biggest thing there was in life, except for business; nothing could stand in the way of business considerations.

On the whole, though, I thought Mary Wright had handled the situation tactfully, and nobody among the game-players seemed to be complaining much, though many were clearly disappointed. And Mary's vague references to the two murders didn't raise any particular questions among them. The police, who had arrived just after one A.M. last night, had questioned a number of the Weekenders—the Arnolds and the Logans among them. The real story had gotten out, over breakfast; hardly fitting table conversation, even at a Mystery Weekend, but what you are going to do?

As the crowd filed out, I stopped Mary and told her I thought she'd handled an impossible task pretty well.

"Thanks, Mal. I still feel numb from last night."

She referred not only to that ill-fated encounter group I'd led in the little lounge, but to the questioning by Chief Colby, which lasted till dawn. Colby, a heavy-set, no-nonsense man, had taken dispassionate charge of the murder scene and sorted out the wild tales and various speculations of myself and others with enviable calm. It was six-thirty A.M. before Jill and I had crawled into the sack; she had dropped right off, but even extreme exhaustion wasn't enough to ease the unpleasant images from my mind. I'd stayed up, tagging along with Colby, till breakfast, where a glass of orange juice had been all I could stomach. Jill was still back in the room asleep right now, most likely.

"I fell pretty washed out myself," I told Mary. "When does the bus leave?"

"Three o'clock this afternoon," she said. "There should be no holdup—the snowplows have been out in force; everything's clear."

"I may skip lunch and catch some sleep. I think I'm finally tired enough to put all this out of mind for a while."

She sighed. "I envy you. I still have to stage-manage what's left of my weekend. Is it crass of me to wonder what will become of our famous Mystery Weekends in the light of this tragedy?"

"Yes," I said.

She let out a rueful little laugh. "You never cut me any slack, do you, Mallory?"

"I try not to," I said, finding a smile for her. "Besides, this isn't a setback."

"No?"

"Of course not. Two murders at the Mohonk Mystery Weekend . . . that'll be big news. Major publicity."

Curt himself had pointed that out.

"You don't think it'll scare people away . . .?"

"Yours is the only mystery weekend ever to deliver the real thing. Don't underestimate the morbidity of the public."

"That sounds like something Kirk Rath might have said."

"It does, doesn't it? I do need some sleep."

"You really admired Curt, didn't you?"

"Yes. I admired his writing, certainly, and always will. And I admired him as a person, until events conspired to unbalance him."

"You feel he was . . . insane?" Her delivery was an unintentional reminder of the TV pitchman, Crazy Eddie.

"All murderers are insane," I shrugged. "Whether

Curt would have been deemed *legally* insane is a question I'm not qualified to answer. And a moot one, at that, thanks to Rick Fahy. Who may be deemed legally insane himself, when the times comes."

Fahy, of course, was in custody; he'd been taken to the holding tank in the New Paltz police station almost immediately after Colby's arrival last night. He hadn't said a word since he'd swung into action; he was silent, seemed as dead, in his way, as Curt. As Rath.

A female staffer in a crisp blue Mohonk blazer approached Mary with a worried look and a question, and I left the social director to her job, and headed for the room, where Jill was indeed still sleeping. I crawled under the covers with her, our twin beds still mating, and sank into sleep.

So deep did I fall that my dreams left me alone, and when I woke, around two, I felt groggy but rested. And, for a moment, I wondered if any of it had really happened. But it only took a moment for reality to assert itself: my shirt from last night, spattered with some of Curt's blood, hung over a nearby chair.

I nudged Jill awake and she took one final shower and so did I, and we packed hurriedly, and soon we were heading down the long hall with our bags in our hands, not fooling around waiting for bellboys.

Before long we had moved out through the cold, clear afternoon, breath smoking, and piled onto the bus. Tom Sardini and Pete Christian were the only fellow suspects of ours aboard, as the Flints were taking the second, later bus. (We hadn't been able to say any good-byes to Tim Culver and Cynthia Crystal; they were staying by Kim's bedside—she was sedated in her room.) Tom and Pete were in the two seats just across the aisle from us, and as the Arnolds climbed on—the last passengers to do so— they paused in the aisle and pointed at Pete.

"You did it," Millie said.

Pete said, "If you're referring to *The Case of the Curious Critic*, I must take the fifth."

"Give us a break," Millie said, pleading, emphatic, red hair tumbling. "You know whether you're the murderer or not."

"Curt's final mystery died with him," was all Pete could say.

Millie turned and looked at me and smiled, embarrassedly. "Do you think I'm terrible to be concerned about how the mystery came out?"

The bus was starting to move; the Victorian man-made cliffs of Mohonk were receding into the background.

"No," I said. "You and all the other teams worked all weekend coming up with your solutions. You put a lot of creative energy into it. I don't blame you for being disappointed."

Curt, it seemed, had not written his solution down; he had planned to deliver it extemporaneously, in his usual freewheeling manner.

"I was afraid you'd think we were terrible," Millie said, like a child pretending she was sorry.

"Not at all," I said cheerfully. "I think you're lunatics, and that's quite another manner."

She took that well, and said, "Most of the teams are in agreement that Pete's character did it. Through process of elimination, he was the only one whose alibi wasn't confirmed, and we caught him in an apparent lie—and only the murderer is allowed to lie, you know. He claimed he hadn't seen the tapes, when we knew that two other witnesses had seen him burning them in an outdoor trash barrel. Besides, his character's last name is 'Butler'—you know, Butler did it? That seems like the sort of cutesy clue Curt Clark might slip in."

"It sure does," I said. "Maybe next year."

"Next year," she said, and moved along. Deadpan

Carl brought up the rear, and he shrugged, and smiled a little, Buster Keaton with a Chaplin mustache.

"How can they think about their stupid mystery?" Jill asked, a bitter edge in her voice.

"Honey, they spent all weekend working on it. I don't blame them. Of course it's eating at them, not knowing for sure who did it. It's like waiting for the other shoe to drop."

Then I leaned across the aisle and said to Pete, "By the way, I know you did it, too."

"Is that right?"

"Yeah. Rick Butler killed Roark Sloth."

"Suppose we did," Pete said, smiling coyly. "Can you prove it?"

"Sure," I said, and leaned across and whispered the solution to him.

"No kidding!" he said. "I should've figured that out myself."

Jill said, "You know how to prove that Pete was the killer in Curt's mystery?"

"Sure."

"How?"

So I whispered it to her: the answer was the cryptic typed message found in the critic's typewriter, TOVL FOF OY. The dying man had placed his hands one key to the right on his typewriter, turning his message into gibberish; by moving the letters on the keyboard back one space to the left, the dying message would read: RICK DID IT.

"Oh my," Jill said. She was making an ironic connection—after all, a man named Rick had killed Curt Clark.

"Yup," I said. "Just as cute and pat as one of Curt's mystery stories."

"And you aren't going to tell the Arnolds or any of the other game-players?"

"What," I said, "and spoil the mystery?"